SUM OF MANY THINGS

a collection by

RICK MALOY

SUM OF MANY THINGS

Published February, 2014 by Seward House.

Copyright © 2014 by Rick Maloy
www.rickmaloy.com

Author services by Pedernales Publishing, LLC.
www.pedernalespublishing.com

Library of Congress Control Number: 2014902247

ISBN 978-0-9896239-3-3 Paperback Edition
ISBN 978-0-9896239-4-0 Digital Edition

Printed in the United States of America

CONTENTS

*To my siblings, who've provided more grist
than I could ever mill.*

ACKNOWLEDGEMENTS

First and always to Steve Lipsitz for encouraging me toward the writing life – despite my painful lack of structure. To my editor, Lynn Skapyak Harlin, whose Shantyboat workshops helped turn three years of literary floundering into a process. Her patience and encyclopedic knowledge of the writing craft were critical in developing the tools necessary to create and self-edit. To Frank Green and his "full contact" critiquing group. Many of their valuable observations have found their way into my work. And last, to my beta readers, Ann Marie Maloy (the Missus) and Pasley Mansfield, neither of whom saw any reason to sugarcoat an opinion.

SUM OF MANY THINGS

MOTHER'S HOME

MAUREEN'S CHEWED FINGERNAILS bumped along a border of the bricked-in fireplace. She tried to imagine her grandparents and their children, including her mother, gathered in front of it. Parents in rockers. Children, lying on their stomachs or sitting cross legged. Reading, playing board games, laughing, glowing. It would have been easier if the stone, two room house hadn't become spray painting booths for an auto repair shop. Hoped-for aromas of hearth fire and farm cooking lay sealed under speckled layers of nostril searing chemicals.

A man behind the counter smiled and raised his eyebrows as she headed for the door. "Not too disappointed, I hope."

"And you're sure this is it?"

"No one's got better records than Kilshanny Pharmacy. If Mr. Mulqueeny says this was your grandfather's place, 'tis the same as hearing it from God himself."

"My mother always speaks of this as 'the farm.' When I told her I was coming over, she made me promise to visit and bring back pictures. I can't. She'd be devastated."

"Ah, well. Things change, don't they. G'day, lass."

Being a thirty-one-year-old "lass" brought a smile as she pushed through the door. The chilling west-Ireland afternoon pattered on the bill of her pink Yankees cap during the dash across the parking lot. Soon as she shut the door of her rental car, a form-fitting Nissan Micra, the rain thickened, slapping at the windscreen at a steep angle.

"Starved." She ripped open a packet of low-fat Oreo Mini's and wedged it between her thighs. A road map covered the passenger seat. She leaned toward it and traced a finger from Kilshanny to the airport at Shannon. Fingers of her other hand tickled into the bag for a treat. "Lahinch Road all the way. One turn in Ennis. How hard can that be?"

"BAREFIELD?" she shouted at the road sign. "How am I going north?" The flattened map crinkled on the steering column. Her eyes flipped from the rain-swept road to the paper. "Okay, Maureen, relax," she said to the rearview. "Plenty of time. Next town's Crusheen. We'll turn around there."

To her left the sky showed a clearly defined edge between marbled grays and unbroken blue. "See? Rain's gonna stop. Oh, and look at this," she told her smiling reflection. "Crusheen. Life is good." She turned into a dead end and chased a sweep of sunshine that electrified the greens and purples of the countryside. A stone house, quite small, stood alone at the end of the lane. In the front yard, a hand-painted B&B sign had been pounded into the lawn at a slight angle.

Her car crunched onto the driveway, backed halfway out, and stopped. She sat forward, nose almost touching the windshield. "How perfect is this? With her eyesight?" One twist of the rearview enabled a quick inspection. She swiped Oreo crumbs from her breasts, fluffed her thick brown waves, and re-glossed her lips. "Good as it gets," she said to the mirror before struggling out of the undersized car. On the driveway, she held a small camera in front of her face and wandered in front of the house. Her eyes stayed fixed on the tiny screen during the walk to the front door. No way her mother would know the difference.

The lion head knocker squeaked each of the three times she lifted it. Chin raised, she pulled back her shoulders. One last finger comb and pat of the hair.

A smiling bird of an old woman in a faded blue and gold housecoat answered. Still holding the doorknob, she shuffled closer to the threshold. Her lumpy finger waggled at the B&B sign. "Mornin', love. Is it a room you're wanting?"

"No, sorry." She smiled and reached out an open hand. "Hi, Maureen Luciano."

The woman glanced down at the extended hand. "Oh, American." She pinched the tips of Maureen's fingers. "Theresa Hanrahan. Missus. Mr. Hanrahan's dead."

"I'm so sorry," Maureen said, feeling instantly ridiculous.

"Yes, three years next Boxing Day." The old woman leaned forward, as if sharing a secret. "Well, at least he got Christmas. And it was a ripping wake." She smiled and stood taller. "So, child, if not a room, what then?"

Maureen pointed back toward the highway. "I got lost and used your driveway to turn around. But then your house. It's so perfect. I just love it."

The old woman's face burst into delight. "Well now, isn't that grand."

"If it's okay with you, I'd like to take a few pictures."

Mrs. Hanrahan tottered backward from the door, one hand on the knob, the other waving her inside. "Take all you like, dear. Cup o' tea? Just having a spot m'self. Another dish at the wash-up's no trouble."

"Thanks," she said, smiling, "but I only need the outside."

Mrs. Hanrahan's arm continued to beckon. "I have family in the states, y'know. Yes, a niece, Bernadette. She's plump like you, but never as pretty. Just outside New York. Teaches at university, I think. Are you from New York?"

"Connecticut." She held up her hands. "You're very generous, Mrs. Hanrahan, but I have a plane to catch. And really, I only need outside shots." She backed down the cinder path. "I'll just walk around out here if that's okay."

"Shannon or Dublin?"

"My flight? Shannon."

The old woman's doughy face compressed. "Oh, you'll be there between that." She clapped her hands and disappeared behind the open door. A clunk of metal echoed inside the little home. "There," she said, back in the doorway, hands clasped in front, "well begun is half done. Tea'll be up by the time you're back. And I have some lovely biscuits. Just come in when you're finished." She leaned into the edge of the door.

"No, really—"

The door clicked shut.

Twenty pictures later, Maureen knocked and eased the

door open. She bent around the edge. "Hello?" The house smelled of peat smoke, tea, and imperfect hygiene.

A beaming Mrs. Hanrahan stood at her wooden dining table. Both hands gripped the top of a slat-back chair. Two settings of white china rested on cranberry linen mats with matching napkins in sterling rings. Steam twisted from the kettle's curved neck. On a plate positioned between the two settings, four shortbread cookies overlapped in a straight line. "Ah, lovely to have a bit o' company. Been ages." She patted a seat that had a view to the distant hills. "Now, you sit there and tell me about yourself," she said, filling two cups with tea.

"This is wonderful of you," Maureen said, one shoulder still outside the door. "But I'm a little manic about getting to airports early. Thank you so much. Such a terrific house."

"Milk?" the woman said, a small pitcher poised over the guest cup.

"Please don't."

Mrs. Hanrahan dumped a small splash into each one. "That's how I take it, too."

Great. Deaf. Like being home.

Silver tongs plucked sugar cubes from an open jar. Mrs. Hanrahan dropped three into Maureen's. "None for me. Bloody doctors," she said as she sat. "So, what brings you to Crusheen, love? Ah yes, you told me. Lost. Sit, child."

"I really can't do this, Mrs.—"

The old woman's eyes squeezed shut. Her lips tightened into a rumpled oval. She dropped onto a chair and fell against the back, fingertips pressed to her chest. Short breaths mixed with groans that puffed through her nose.

"Omigod. Mrs. Hanrahan?" Maureen shut the door behind her and hurried to the table. On one knee she took a flimsy hand into both of hers. "Are you alright? Should I call someone?"

A quick shake of the head. The woman's other hand covered Maureen's and gripped it surprisingly tight. Her breathing slowed and deepened. Face and clutch relaxed. Eyes blinked a few times before seeming to recognize anything. "Just one of me spells, dear." She offered a thin smile and pointed toward the sink. "I've some pills back there, if it's not a bother. There's a good girl."

Bronze pharmacy bottles lined a grungy strip of counter between the tin back splash and the faucets.

"Which one?" Maureen asked, reluctant to touch anything.

"Should say nitro glycerin. One will do."

Maureen twisted the cap off, handed her the bottle, and stood in waiting. "I don't want to leave you like this. Please, let me phone someone before I go."

Mrs. Hanrahan patted her on the hand. "Sit, lass." She shook a tiny pill from the bottle and placed it under her tongue. "Must have overdone it a bit is all. Finish your tea, dear. You've plenty of time."

"Are you sure I can't phone someone?" She hung her purse on the back of the chair and lowered onto the edge of the seat. "A relative? Your doctor?"

"Just the tonic, that nitro glycerin." Mrs. Hanrahan tapped herself on the chest. "Better already. Have a biscuit, child."

"I really shouldn't." Time was getting away from her, but a few more minutes would let her leave without feeling guilty. "They do look yummy." She broke a cookie in half and nipped off a corner. "Omigod. Sinful." After another nibble, she picked the other half off the plate.

"Ah, lovely to see a young woman enjoy food. So many try to look like greyhounds these days. And the lads appreciate a bit of roundness, I think. Are you married, child?"

"Not yet."

"Engaged then?"

She shook her head.

"A steady?"

"Not at the moment."

"Ah, well. You're young yet. And so pretty."

Familiar tension built inside her, a feeling usually reserved for Sundays, after dinner with the family, after her older sister, brother-in-law and their four kids went home. Every week, while she helped her mother clean the kitchen, her status was discussed – replete with suggestions – until she escaped to her room with a book. The major difference here was being "pretty."

"This has been very nice, Mrs. Hanrahan. Really." She twisted sideways in the chair and lifted the purse strap. "But I have to get going now."

"Just like Angela," the old woman said, her cloudy blue eyes gone glassy. "Life's great adventure, tugging you away, making you bold. God's sorrowful plan for mothers, I suppose."

"Angela's your daughter?" She stayed seated, purse propped on her knees.

Nodding her head slowly, Mrs. Hanrahan blessed

herself. "She's with the Lord. Thirty-four years come July third."

"Oh, I'm so sorry." This time the sympathy was genuine.

"Killed on holiday in Majorca. A lad she met there ran their motorbike into a stone wall. That's her there." The old woman pointed to an eight-by-ten black and white photograph hanging on the whitewashed wall, ancient palm fronds drooping from the top of the frame. "That's my Angela."

Maureen circled behind Mrs. Hanrahan's chair and approached the picture, half expecting to see herself.

"That's a year before she died."

The portrait was a partial profile. Aside from the dark, wavy hair, she saw no resemblance. Angela's face was rounder, eyes smaller, nose stubbier. The flurry of freckles meant her skin was fairer, maybe even pasty. Large, unharnessed teeth gleamed through lips pulled thin by a wide smile. The edge of an earlobe peeked through thick, mid-neck hair.

"You must miss her terribly," she said, still studying the homely face. When Mrs. Hanrahan didn't answer, she turned. "Especially—"

Eyes shut, hands flat on her chest, the old woman was frozen in a silent scream.

"Dear God." Maureen raced to her side. "Another nitro?"

Breaths started again, rapid and shallow. She shook her head.

"A doctor? Do you need a doctor?"

This time a nod. "Nine, nine, nine," came out in gasps.

"That's Emergency? Nine, nine, nine?"

Nodding again, Mrs. Hanrahan pointed to the counter by the small fridge.

Maureen ran to the rotary phone and dialed the number.

"Emergency," a young-sounding female said.

"Send an ambulance. There's an elderly woman. I think it's her heart."

"Address is coming up eleven twenty-six Inchicronin, in Crusheen. Is that where the ambulance is needed?"

"I don't know. Probably. This isn't my house. Please hurry. She took a nitro glycerin, but it's not helping."

"They've been dispatched, madam."

Back beside Mrs. Hanrahan's chair, she rested her hand lightly on the old woman's back. "They're coming. Can I phone anyone else?"

Nose wrinkled, Mrs. Hanrahan pointed to the open bedroom door. "Best lie down." A little smile flashed between the groans. "Undertaker'll charge extra if I break me face." Her arms reached like a baby. "Would you mind, love?"

God, what am I doing here?

She spread a light blanket over Mrs. Hanrahan and pulled a ladder-back chair to the side of the double bed. "Can I get you anything?" she said, stroking the back of the woman's hand.

"Now who put these here?" Mrs. Hanrahan smiled and swiped at tears dribbling toward her ears. "Perhaps a tissue, dear."

She stripped a few from a box on the nightstand and pressed them into the boney hand. "Is it the pain?"

"Nay." She dabbed the bundle at some new leakage.

"Can be a great sadness at times, understanding so much when it doesn't matter anymore."

Please don't die on me.

Mrs. Hanrahan's eyes met hers. "Oh, such a face," she said through a thin smile. " 'Tis why we're born, child. A bit of God's mischief, letting us muck about in the dark most of the time. But no one's taken 'til they're ready." She ran a finger over Maureen's hand and closed her eyes again. "Let's have no more of it. So, tell me then, have you a profession?"

"I'm a teacher. Second grade."

"Ah, so you're around the little ones. That's grand. Parish school?"

"Catholic schools don't pay enough." She checked her watch. "Shouldn't they be here by now?"

The grip tightened. "Please don't leave me."

"Sssh." Maureen squeezed back. "I won't. Just wondered if you think I should call again."

Using her free hand, Mrs. Hanrahan tapped the wad of tissues into the corner of each eye. "You've missed it, haven't you? I'm so sorry, child."

"Probably. Guess I'll get a room near the airport and go out tomorrow if there's space."

"Rubbish. You'll stay here."

"I couldn't."

"Course you can. You're in a B&B, dear. The services will be a bit spare, like me funeral," she said with a small laugh, "but the price is right."

A vehicle arrived in front of the house, engine running. Orange and white lights flashed through the window and repeated across the walls.

She let go of the old woman's hand and hurried toward the squeak and clank of the knocker.

"I'd rather the place show some life 'til I'm back, love," Mrs. Hanrahan called after her.

Teeth clenched, she reached the door just as a woman in matching blue shirt and slacks opened it and leaned inside.

"Call for an ambulance, Miss?"

"In there," she said, pointing toward the open bedroom door.

"If that's your car, Miss," the attendant said on her way past, "would you mind awfully if I asked you to move it?"

Rental car safely out of the way, Maureen rested her hips against the driver's door and gazed up. Returning clouds had coated the sky with dullness, chilled the air. She hugged herself and waited.

A second female attendant backed the ambulance up cinder tracks in the weedy driveway. She opened the back, removed a gurney, and wheeled it into the house.

Arms still tight around her middle, Maureen's slow, weaving steps carried her up the driveway, stopping near the ambulance's side mirror.

Only a short time passed before the EMT's rolled Mrs. Hanrahan out the front door, an oxygen line clipped to her nose.

"Hope everything's okay," Maureen called to the old woman. "Don't worry about anything here. I'll lock up when I leave." *Although I'm not sure how.*

The attendant who'd spoken to her in the house approached the driver's door. "I think she's fine, Miss. Vitals are good." She shook a plastic bag full of prescription bottles. "Might've knocked herself all sixes and sevens with these again."

"Same with my mother. I have to— 'Again'? You know her?"

"Been here at least once this year," the woman said as she hoisted herself into the driver's seat. She started the engine. "Might be twice. I think the old ones call sometimes because they're lonely. Still, you were right to ring us. Mind your feet, Miss," she said as the ambulance rolled toward the street.

Drops of new rain slapped dark circles in the cinders as flashing lights headed away at an unhurried pace.

Back inside, she wandered the small house, stopping every few paces to examine something in the dimming light. An empty candy dish. Cobwebs between the fireplace tools. A pewter statue of Jesus on a shelf of honor, standing guard over the charred wick of a long-gone votive candle. A spray of dried periwinkle and bridal wreath, bound by a faded pink ribbon, hung upside down on the door of tonight's bedroom.

Seated at her place at the table, chin propped on her knuckles, she watched the countryside fade and disappear in the strengthening rain. She snapped a cookie in half, nibbled until it was gone. Did it again. Did it until all the halves were gone. She shuttled the dishes to the sink, washed and dried them. Stripping gunk from behind the faucets took more effort than she expected, but she stayed at it until the circles left by the pill bottles were gone.

"Deserve a little something." She opened and closed cabinet doors until finding the biscuit tin. Cover off, she cradled it in one arm and roamed the house again.

In Mrs. Hanrahan's room, she decided to make the bed. Framed pictures and religious curios crowded the top of a small dresser, so she opened a drawer and laid the tin on some clothing. She squared and tucked the corners of the blanket, stretched across the bed for a final smoothing. Her hands ran over side-by-side depressions in the mattress. The history of a couple. Parents popped into her head, then just her father, gone over twenty years. Her poor mother, a widow for so long. But at least there were ruts in her bed.

The movie of her life raced to the credits. She saw the house back in Connecticut, the one she lived in, grew up in. It was her mother's home. All she had was a room and chores, and on some not-too-distant day, one of those chores would resemble today. Hold her mother's hand while she died. Minister, soothe, and ease the exit. Her busy sister couldn't do it. Shouldn't have to. The responsibility came with the tenancy.

Then what? Move into her mother's room? Live out her time in her mother's home? Each year, the school children would stay the same age, but she'd be older. One day it would be time for her hand to be held. Who would do that? She dropped onto the side chair. Sobs exploded into cupped hands.

Feeling dizzy in the dark of her hands, she slowed her breathing until the storm spent itself. Steady on her feet, she ripped tissues from the box on the nightstand and pressed them to her eyes as she scuffed to the dresser to reclaim the biscuits.

Cookie tin cradled in the crook of her arm, she wandered back into the main room and found herself in front of Angela's portrait once more. Such a hopeful smile.

A rising life. Daring enough to venture to an exotic place. Spread her legs over a motorbike. Die glamorously before understanding too much.

While she imagined the short life, biscuits disappeared fragment by fragment, until all that remained were crumbs she sucked from the tip of a moistened finger.

LEAVING THE BAND

WES BOUNCED and twisted in the passenger seat but couldn't get comfortable. He opened his pickup's glove compartment and propped a yellow pad on the open door. Draped around his acoustic, he strummed and tickled counterpoint with his pinky while he sang the lyrics he'd written during lunch break. "Sucks!" He thwanged a pick across the strings. "Sorry," he said, patting and stroking the body. After he'd steadied the guitar in the driver's seat, he snatched the pad, grabbed a ballpoint from over his ear, and slashed through his words until the pen snapped.

Boots propped on the dash, he stared across the parking lot, at the door to their apartment. A phone buzzed in a front pocket of his jeans. "Blow it out your fat ass," he said as he dug it out. *Sled Dog* on the caller I.D. made him smile. "About time, asshole" he shouted into the mouthpiece.

"Wes, if that message is bullshit, I swear, I'll cut out your heart and make you eat it."

"No bullshit, buddy. Manny booked us into Star Maker. Slobberknocker's headed for Hollywood. Didn't I tell you?" he screamed over Sled Dog's war whoops. "Our own shit. Gotta do our own shit. Get it tight. I could feel it. Didn't I say it was getting tight?"

"Dude, I'm busting. How much we talking about?"

He flinched and covered his eyes. "Not about money. It's about getting in front of the right people."

"Okay, how much *aren't* we talking about?"

"Star Maker doesn't pay the talent."

"Godammit, Wes." Snorted breaths gusted through the receiver. "Gonna grab Manny by the ankles and beat you to death with him. How could you agree to that?"

"This is our shot, man. *Mouth Breather X15, Billy's Bad Hair Day, Middle Diddle.* They all came through there. Everyone knows these guys only book the best. It's our ticket, and we're taking the ride."

"Sounds like your voice, dude, but I'm hearing Manny. You don't know shit about this club, do you?"

"Know what, Sled Dog? You don't want to go? Don't go."

"Dude, back off."

"No. Manny told me if any of you have a problem, he can get studio guys. How hard you think it is to find another bass?"

"Cut the diva crap, Wes. You're talking to me. And I didn't say no … What's the airfare?"

"Doesn't matter. Only Rico and Flatline are flying. You and I are driving Rico's van. That way we can take all our stuff. Even the drums."

"Bullshit. It's Rico's van. You and him drive, and I'll fly."

"Neither of them can get out of work. We can."

"Two of us? Driving from St. Augustine to L.A.? Dude, it's gotta be three thousand miles."

"Two thousand, three hundred and fifty-three. Already printed the map from Google. Less than three days each way if we share the driving. I figure with meals and a hotel in L.A., we can last ten days for about five hundred each. At least that's what I told Belinda."

"Damn, talk about bad timing. She okay with this?"

"Not exactly." He glanced toward the apartment, shifted sideways in the seat, and pressed his back against the door. "Right after Manny called today, I phoned her. Thought she'd be all proud and stuff. Hung up on me."

"But you're still going?"

"Sled Dog, I've been grinding eleven years for this. Been a husband for four months and a father for five weeks. Seems to me it'd be a whole lot easier getting another wife and baby than a second shot at Star Maker. Hell yes, I'm going."

"Are you home?"

"Sitting in my truck out front." His eyes drifted back to the apartment door. "Trying to write some new stuff. If I play or listen inside, I'm disturbing the baby. If I put the earphones in, I'm ignoring her. Playing with you dirtbags is about the only fun I have anymore."

"Dude," Sled Dog said, laughing, "maybe we'll make it big, and you can hang outside the apartment in a big-ass RV."

"Sounds good to me. Hey, I'll call you later. Probably holding up dinner, and eating's about the only thing she seems to enjoy these days."

The apartment door clicked behind him. He set his guitar case down. "Hey," he said, along with a half wave. "Something smells good. Italian what?"

Belinda kicked out of a recliner, closed a magazine, and spun it onto the seat cushion. "You're late. Water's been boiling for ten minutes." She flicked her eyes at him once, tilted her head back, and strutted to the stove.

"Still mad, I see." He tiptoed to the bassinet next to the dining table and leaned over. "Hey there, Hope. Were you a good—"

"Leave her."

He spread his arms. "Why the hell you so mad? You knew this could happen if the right things showed up."

Fussing started in the bassinet. Belinda moved him aside with a hand against his chest. "Dammit, just had her quiet." She stuck a pacifier back in and smoothed the blanket. "There you go, sweetie. Poor little Hope, probably crying because she knows insanity's hereditary."

He trailed Belinda as she headed back to the stove. "That's it? I'm crazy? I've been working a long time for this. Gimme something here."

She snapped handfuls of spaghetti in half, threw them in the pot, and spun toward him. "Like what? Congratulations for letting Manny make a jackass out of you again? You're gonna disappear for two weeks—"

"Wrong. I said ten days. Maybe eleven."

"Wes," she said, her open hands pushing at him, "we're not talking about this now. I got things to do."

Both stayed quiet while she tended the pots on the stove, stirring one and tasting from the other. She banged a wooden spoon against the edge of the marinara pot, handed him a strainer, and pointed to the sink. "So, you want to be gone for eleven days, and spend two thousand dollars we don't—"

"No. You didn't hear that right either. It's two thousand for the whole group. That's only five hundred each."

Spaghetti dangled from the spoon. She ate a strand and turned off the burners. "Okay, so you want to spend five hundred we don't have, to go to Los Angeles for one show that pays nothing." She lugged the pot to the sink. "Watch your hands."

He backed his head away as pasta, water, and steam spilled into the colander. "This could be big. Manny said the guy went insane over our demo."

"Manny's a liar and a thief." She took the strainer from him and ran water over the noodles. "Where's the thousand dollars he already owes you? And what guy — other than you — went insane?"

"The guy Manny sent our CD to. The manager of Star Maker. That's where we're booked. Manny said the guy went nuts. Said we have a unique sound. Could be huge if we get it out there first."

"Wes, you're the one with the unique sound. Your songs, your vocals, your lead guitar. Maybe if even one of the other guys had any talent, Slobberknocker would've gotten somewhere by now."

"You don't know what you're talking about. And we're booked the way we are. That's it. Least for now." He grabbed a bottle of beer from the sparse contents in the fridge. "Want one?" He shrugged at her slow shake of the head and raised the bottle over his head. "Here's to you, Wesley Carnes. Good for you, boy." The beer disappeared in a single tip. He burbled out a long belch, grabbed a replacement bottle, and waited near the table. "At least let me tell you what I was gonna say before you hung up."

Eyes forward, she passed him and set the plates of spaghetti on the table.

"What am I doing?" he said, barely above a whisper.

She turned and studied his face. "Tell me while we eat."

"Okay." He raced to his chair but didn't sit. "So, Manny said he sent out the demo disc only yesterday and the guy called him *today*. Said he listened to it five times straight. Couldn't believe how good we are. Gave us his first available slot. Manny called me as soon as he got off the phone with the guy." He took a quick sip of the beer. "I gotta say, I thought you'd be happy."

"You are crazy." She sat and rocked her hips as she spread a napkin on her lap. Nose wrinkled, she kept her eyes on the pasta and swirled on red sauce from a small pitcher. "Why do you need ten days for one show? You said the drive's three. That's three days there, one to do the show, and three back." She dinged her fork on his plate. "Gonna get cold."

He sat, knees spread, forearms resting on the table. "Manny's trying to get us more spots out there. First we do Star Maker, then we do other clubs. Y'know, build on the buzz." He lowered one eyelid and fired his index finger at her. "And those we get paid for. If he finds any, that is."

She sniffed at the shaker of grated parmesan, closed her eyes, and smiled. "So, tell me again. When's this supposed to happen?"

"Week from Saturday."

"A Saturday show. At least that's good."

He cleared his throat. "Actually, show's on Tuesday. We're leaving Saturday."

Her eyes and mouth popped wide. She bent over her food and laughed. "A Tuesday show? And where are you on the bill?"

"We open, but don't—"

"Opening? On a Tuesday? This gets more idiotic by the minute. He might as well have booked you into the Bowl-A-Rama in Crescent Beach."

"Stop acting like you're some kind of expert on the goddam business, Belinda. Starting to piss me off. L.A. isn't like here. Nothing like Star Maker in all of Florida. Probably not even in Atlanta. You don't get into this place unless you have the magic."

"Do me a favor," she said, turning her frown away from him, "don't use Manny-isms around me. 'The magic.' What's next? Every lottery has a winner?"

"Well, that's true, isn't it? And why not us? Every group you ever heard on the radio started like this."

"And what about your job?" she said, leaning a wide smile at him. "Gonna call in sick for ten days?"

He dropped his gaze to the table. "I'm gonna, y'know, use my vacation."

"What about Tybee Island?"

Angling away from her, he crossed his legs. "So, I'm supposed to tell the break that's been ducking me for eleven years, 'Catch me some other time. I got this week at Tybee goddam Island.' That what you're saying?"

"It's our honeymoon. Wes, dreaming about being a rock star is okay for kids. Twenty-six isn't a kid any more. You've got a family now. And it's a pure mystery to me how you can still be falling for Manny's line of crap." She leaned toward him. "You win one Battle of the Bands, at a mostly empty race track, and that huckster has you convinced you're the next Green friggin' Day. Last I heard, Green Day gets paid." She poked her fork into the pasta and twirled a big knot against her spoon. "Shouldn't be chasing his stupid ideas to California." A man-of-war of spaghetti hovered in front of her mouth. "Should have that slimeball arrested." She snatched at the food. Spinning strands slurped through her lips.

His face tightened after a peek at the hips spilling over her molded chair.

"Got something to say?" she said, repositioning herself in the seat.

"We'll get the money." He pushed the plate away and thumped his fingers on the empty spot. "Y'know, we did beat seven other groups that night."

"I was there, remember? Bunch of high school head-bangers."

"Couple of them were pretty good. And we won. That's something. Why you dumping on this now? You were plenty happy back then."

"I thought we won a thousand dollars."

He leaned back, but bounced forward again. "And the crowd was small because the forecast called for thunderstorms."

"Let's see." She tapped a finger against her chin and gazed at the ceiling. "Thunderstorms, in Florida, in July. Hmmm."

He downed the rest of his beer and headed to the refrigerator. "Belinda? Suck it."

Her flat hand slamming on the table jangled the dishes and silverware. Crying erupted from the bassinet. "You do not speak like that in this house. Not to me, and not in front of Hope. Y'hear me?"

Empty-handed, he shut the fridge door and weaved

toward her. "Well then," he said bending so they were nose to nose, "enjoy the quiet." Returning her glare, he headed for the door. Halfway out he reached back inside and grabbed his guitar case.

"WAS A MISTAKE to marry her," Wes said from the driver's seat. "Think so?"

"You talking to me?" Sled Dog said, laughing. "Dude, you don't say a word for like, I dunno, a day, and that's what you open with?"

"No one else in the damn van."

"I ain't real smart, Wes, but I'm not getting into one of *those* conversations." He changed the radio station. "Good idea last night, staying in that motel. We'll have plenty of energy when we get there. Whadaya figure? Three o'clock?"

"She told me I didn't have to. Said she'd be okay."

"Man, talk to her about her, not me. Have you even called yet?"

"Nope."

"She call you?"

"Once. About an hour after I left. Saw it was her and let it go to voicemail."

"Dude, that's not right."

"Still there. I'll listen to it after we do the show."

"Why the hell you waiting?"

He slouched against the door and rubbed his chin. "Not sure, exactly. It's like I gotta be one thing or the other right now. I'm out here for my music, and I'm, y'know, not being serious if I let family stuff get in the way. Know what I'm saying?"

"Not even a little. By the way, what's this guy's name?"

"Who?"

"The Star Maker guy."

Wes wrinkled his brow, drummed fingers on the wheel. "Actually? I don't know. Can't remember Manny calling him anything but 'the guy.'" He shrugged. "But the guy knows us. We'll just ask for the manager."

"For crissake, man." Sled Dog had crying in his voice. "Get some details once in a while."

"You want to know?" he said, tossing his phone. "Call Manny."

Sled Dog dialed, held the phone to his ear, and cleared his throat. "Yeah, Manny, it's Sled Dog from Slobberknocker. We're about eighty miles from L.A. and need some info on the Star Maker gig. Call Wes's cell soon as you can. Later."

"So," he said, reaching for his phone, "you're 'Sled Dog from Slobberknocker'. Not some other Sled Dog."

"Wow, you're right. We make it big, Wes? I could be a one-word guy, like Sting or Bono. Famous as hell, and no one ever knows my real name. How *epic* would that be?"

"Sled Dog's two words."

"Not anymore."

A CENTER ISLAND of giant palm trees separated the lanes of traffic. "There it is." Sled Dog backhanded him on the shoulder. "Dude, where the hell you going?"

He tried to follow his friend's point. "You see it?"

"Across the divider. You blind? You just passed it."

He caught a glimpse out the window, then found it in the side mirror. "No. That little shithole?"

"You mean the one with the big-ass Star Maker sign on the fifty-foot pole? Yeah, I'm thinking that might be it."

"Can't be. Gotta be behind that somewhere." He u-turned at the next light. Tires crunched on gravel as they glided through the curb-cut and stopped directly under the sign. Only two other cars sat in the sprawling lot. They got out, stretched, and looked around as they walked to the back of the van. "Kinda like the picture on the website," Wes said, pointing to the windowless, stucco building, "but I was expecting something huge. This wouldn't make a good diner."

"Wes, check it out." Grinning, Sled Dog pointed to the electronic crawl on the bottom of the billboard. Standing side by side, they alternately smiled at each other or followed the moving letters.

Tuesday!!! … First show 9:00 PM … Pretty in Punk … Bed Pan … and introducing …

Fist punches.

… Cranky Bitches … Ticket office opens 5:00PM … Tuesday!!! … First show9:00 PM … Pretty in Punk …

They exchanged open-mouthed stares. "Dude," Sled Dog said, head angled, "you sure he said this Tuesday?"

Wes sanded his hands against the back pockets of his jeans, flexed his jaw muscles. "They must've forgot to change the sign," he said, bobbing his chin toward the building. "Let's check it out."

"It's only 3:35. Sign said it opens at 5:00."

"There's cars. Has to be people. C'mon. And maybe we should call Manny again."

Inside the lobby, every surface was painted black. The only light came from an exit sign. They wandered in the pink gloom while their eyes adjusted. "Here's something," Wes said. Next to the window for ticket sales, he pushed a white button under a tiny *Ring for Service* sign.

A woman entered the booth through a side door and flipped on a light. She hooded her eyes and peered through the inch-thick glass. "Can I help you?" she said, bending to a microphone.

He pressed their business card against the window. "We're Slobberknocker. You the manager?"

Head shaking, she pulled a lever. A drawer telescoped toward him. "Drop the card in there." After it came back to her, she disappeared through the side door.

"Dude, I got a bad feeling."

"Shut up." He pulled out his cell and called Manny. Voicemail. Teeth clenched, he cocked his arm and aimed the phone at the glass. He pumped once, then again. Slowly, his arm lowered to his side. Cell back in his pocket, he dug fingers into his forehead and paced in front of the window.

A beefy man with a gray pony-tail came into the ticket booth and stooped to the mic. "You guys have to talk to your manager. You're not going on."

"Bullshit." Both of Wes's hands slapped onto the window.

"Back off, pal. He never sent the promotion money. Thousand bucks. Had to be here three days ago. It never showed, so I booked someone else. That's it." He turned his back, shut off the light, and left the booth.

"Making a mistake," Wes shouted. One hand beat on the window, the other pumped at the button. "I know he sent it. He had to send it."

A hand shook his shoulder. "Wes, what the hell is he talking about? 'Promotion money.'"

He kept his back to Sled Dog. "We don't have a local following, so we had to agree to pay for some advertising." He went back to hammering the glass and pumping his thumb on the button. "Gotta get that guy back out here. I'll pay the thousand myself."

"Dude … Dude … Wes!"

"What?" he said, his arm frozen on the glass.

"How?"

"How what? How could I give everyone's share to Manny?"

"No, I kinda understand that. I mean how you gonna pay the thousand? She canceled your cards before we got out of Alabama. I'm okay buying your clothes and most of the trip, but Manny money? NFW, dude."

"This is me, Sled Dog. You know I'm good for it."

"All these guys are the same, Wes. Don't you see?" He pointed at the glass. "I wouldn't trust him any more than I trust Manny. C'mon, let's haul our asses back to Florida, find that scumbag, and tie his neck to a train track."

He spun toward Sled Dog. "I'm not leaving until I get on that stage. Our sound got us booked here. Wasn't Manny. Wasn't the thousand dollars. It was the demo. Eleven years of fitting it all together. Writing. Rehearsing. All the shitty jobs."

Sled Dog scratched the back of his head. "Why would that jackass let us take the ride if he wasn't going to send the money? He's gotta know we'll hunt him down."

"Probably thought he could bullshit his way through. Like always. Or one of us would pay it. What I do know is I belong here, and I'm going on tomorrow night."

"Dude, are you deaf? Ponytail-guy booked somebody else. Look, you can stay, but I'm going home."

"I meant all of us. We belong here. Tonight, after Rico and Flatline get in, we'll come back here, remind that guy about the demo. Then I'll get one of them to cough over the money."

"Back up a second. Who told you the guy loved the demo? Manny. What makes you so sure the guy even heard it?"

"We're already here, man. Can't just give up. Might be our one chance."

"Jesus Christ. Pay attention for once. It's not our chance anymore. It's Cranky Bitches' chance. No wonder Manny can twist you so easy. Dude, you're hopeless."

He laced fingers on top of his head and tipped his face to the ceiling. "Hopeless," he said softly, eyes closed.

"Y'okay?"

"I'll meet you outside."

"Sorry, Wes. It's just that sometimes—"

"I know… I know." He pointed at the door. "Couple minutes."

"No problem, but leave the damn bell alone. This round's over." Sled Dog held out his hand. "Keys. I'll get the A.C. going." Sunlight washed in and out of the lobby as Sled Dog left.

He called his mailbox and retrieved Belinda's message. Free hand cupping an ear, he leaned back against the wall.

"Wes," she said in a calm voice, "I'm not calling to say I'm sorry, because I have nothing to be sorry about. I wasn't ridiculing your dreams for Slobberknocker."

"Bullshit."

"I was trying to get you to understand you're part of a family now. That means your needs come last. Same as me. That's how people live valuable lives. It's a little after nine right now, and the real reason I'm calling is to tell you that if you don't come home tonight, don't bother at all. If I let you do this once, it'll happen again. That's not how I'm going to live my life. I don't want you to phone. Just come home to me and Hope. We love you. Bye."

He powered off and sagged to the floor, legs folded underneath lotus-style. Bending forward, he brushed the warm phone across his lips and cheek, tapped it against his forehead like the hammer of a striking clock.

The van was waiting for him outside the door, engine running. Sled Dog lowered the window. "Jump in. I'll take the first two hundred miles."

"I'm not going."

Sled Dog slapped himself on the forehead. "Dude, snap out of it. Got no place to stay, no money, and no credit card. Hop in. We're losing all the cool air."

"You still have cards. Gimme your cash, then stop somewhere and get some more."

Forehead wrinkled, Sled Dog slowly shook his head. "Not happening. Let's go."

Wes held out his phone and rocked it. "Nothing back there for me anymore."

"You finally talked to her?"

"Listened to the message," he said. "I'm a free agent. She told me not to come back."

Laughing, Sled Dog stretched across the center console and pushed the passenger door open. "Women love saying shit like that. Get in."

They hadn't driven three minutes when Wes saw the *Super 8* sign on the right. "Yeah, there it is. Pull into that motel."

"Restaurants are better if you have to piss."

"No, right here's good." The van stopped in front of the office. He stared through the windshield until the words lined up right. "Remember asking me why I hadn't called her, and I said I gotta be one thing or the other?"

"Sorta."

"I know what that one thing is now. I'm out and I'm staying out." He jumped from the van, slid the side door open, and piled his things onto the cracked pavement. One duffel bag, one briefcase full of music, one laptop, and two guitars.

"How you gonna pay for the room?"

"I'll think of something."

"Wes, don't do this. People back there need you. There's no Slobberknocker without you."

He walked around to the driver's window and laid his arms on the roof. "I know who you really mean."

"There's a lot worse, dude. Trust me."

His face hung lower than his shoulders. "This is going to sound bad, but all I care about is the music. Haven't missed either one of them. Not for one second. They're like faces in a crowd scene. And then that message. Holy crap. I heard that and saw myself as this ... guy. Baby carrier in one hand, diaper bag in the other. Trailing his fat wife through IHOP on Sunday morning. I can't be that. I just can't. I'm saving three lives staying out here."

Sled Dog's fist thumped time on the steering wheel. "And what are they supposed to do?"

"She told me not to come back, so she must have some kind of plan." He punched his friend's shoulder. "Why don't you marry her? Least I'd look good next to somebody."

"How you gonna live?" Sled Dog stared out the windshield.

He shrugged. "Pawn one of the guitars for a start. Then find a place. Get some kind of job. Sniff around for a new group. See who likes my songs." He bounced his shoulders again. "I'll be okay."

"Probably shouldn't." Sled Dog raised his hips off the seat and dug fistfuls of crushed bills from the pockets of his jeans. He made a nest of them and handed it out the window. "Best I can do."

"Thanks, man. Y' know," he said, stuffing the cash into his front pockets, "you're not due anywhere for another week. Why don't you stay, too? See how it feels."

"Can't," he said, pointing to Wes's pockets. "Outta money." He wrinkled his nose. "Tell you the truth, I wasn't real disappointed about the screw-up at Star Maker. You belong there. Slobberknocker doesn't. We just tried to keep time and stay out of the way." He stuck his fist out the window. "Enjoyed the ride, buddy. Kick some ass out here."

They banged knuckles and the van headed for the exit.

"Sled Dog, wait!" He jogged to the driver's window. "Would you call the other guys and give 'em the bad news? I'm not really up for that right now."

Sled Dog snorted a laugh and shook his head. "Never noticed before, Wes, but you got some Manny in you."

"C'mon, cut me a break here. Dealing with a plateful of shit right now. One last favor."

"Sure. Whatever." The van rolled a few inches and

stopped. "Just curious. You gonna be Slobberknocker out here?"

"Nah. You guys can have that. Probably need something more Hollywood." He slapped the roof of the van and backed away. "Face in a Crowd Scene sounded pretty good a minute ago. Maybe I'll be that."

STUCK IN DESTIN

"WOW, KINDA SHAKY. Sure you won't mind if I sit for a second, Graham.

"That's better. Ground's damp. Hope it's just dew.

"So, you old rascal, surprised I found you? Piece of cake really. Got a friend who's with the FBI. Took him less than ten minutes to give me your address, plus all kinds of good stuff. Your second DWI last year, for instance. No big surprise there, right? I mean, how many times did I watch you and my Adrianna get loaded at parties? Dancing all dirty-like. Pawing each other. Her giggling and telling me to mind my own business. Should've seen where that was headed, but …

"So, let's see, what else? Oh yeah, you been in Destin two years. Pretty community, by the way. But I'd have to guess that with your wife dead and no license, this place must have felt like death row with palm trees. But like I said, it is lovely. Good as any if you gotta be stuck somewhere.

"Unlikely reunion, huh? Actually, it was Adrianna's last wish. Bet you didn't even know she died. Week ago Tuesday. Near the end, she made me promise to find you and give you this letter. Like always, I said yes, and if you tell a dying person you'll do something, you have to do it. But can you believe her? Walks out on me after eleven years, then has the nerve to ask this?

"My own fault, really. When she took off for Vegas, I shouldn't have followed. She said it showed how weak I am, why she couldn't be with me anymore, but I didn't care. Love can make a person crazy sometimes.

"God, there was magic in that woman, wasn't there? Makes me smile right now just thinking about her. Wild child. Life at double speed. Probably why she didn't make fifty.

"Anyway, once she died, I opened the letter. Wonder if she thought I wouldn't? Maybe thought she could still boss me, even from the grave. Kinda wish I hadn't now, but what the hell. Here, I'll read it to you.

Dearest Graham,

In all these years, not a day's gone by that I haven't been warmed by some memory of you. Something you did that was thoughtful, or tender, or funny. Like no one in my life, you knew me, accepted me, touched me.

When you read this, I'll be gone. I'm sending it to tell you three things.

First, you were the great passion of my life, and I will love you forever.

Second, I've always understood why you never came to me.

And last, I forgive you.

"Then, of course, she signed it. Can't see it in this light, but it's beautiful handwriting.

"Probably read this damn thing a hundred times now. Always makes me mad. She forgives you. You get her to walk out on me, leave town, and then you don't show up. You keep your family, your job, your friends, your whole goddam happy life. She ends up a boozy waitress at a casino. How does she forgive that? How can she still love a maggot like you after nine years? I spent that whole time working to get her back, being a shoulder for her troubles. Never made love to her once. I was the one who took care of her through two cancers, watched her wither and die. I bury her, but you get the goddam love letter. She calls a piece of trash like you her 'great passion.' What could you have possibly said or done in those few months to deserve such a gift?

"Told you I shouldn't have read it. Does this to me every time. It's just hard to think how easy you had it. Somebody had to make you pay.

"Tonight, on the ride down here I laughed out loud when I thought about Adrianna making me find you. She probably had some picture of me handing you the letter, watching you read it. We'd break down together. I'd, y'know, pat you on the shoulder or something, then walk away. She'd be plenty surprised now, I promise you. Maybe even impressed.

"Smells like rain.

"Oh, hey, you'll love this. Know how I got through your crackerjack security? Told the old guy in the booth I wanted to buy a shirt at your pro shop. He smiled, slipped a pass on my dashboard, and raised that useless gate. Already knew the whole layout from a map on the Internet. Parked down the street from your house and waited. Just before dark, I watched you waddle out the front door. Followed you along the path that goes through this dinky nature preserve. Saw you drag your useless carcass into the clubhouse, sit at the bar, and stuff your fat face. Left while you were signing the check. Waited for you right over there.

"Might be wrong about the rain. Just saw some stars.

"Well, I'm gonna take off. Sorry about my foot on your ear, but this concrete head of yours won't give me back my screwdriver. Probably should've used a Philip's. Maybe a twist with the pull. There we go.

"Okay, buddy, time for a swim. God *damn* you got fat. Gonna burn like a tire fire in hell. Have to roll you, I guess.

"And one more.

"Okay, a little shove and *bon voyage*.

"Maybe I'll see you down there."

SEEING THINGS

A KEY CHATTERED in the lock. Tommy lowered the binoculars and eyeballed the door.

Barbara Jean shouldered into their tiny apartment, a bag of groceries in her arm. Trails of sweat glittered on her neck and blotchy round face. Key clamped in her teeth, she squatted for a second bag, showing all of her flowery tramp-stamp and an inch of butt crack. She hipped the door shut and ran in a hunch toward the kitchen counter. One of the collapsing bags didn't make it. "Shit!" Cans of soup bumbled across the floor, stopping under the leg platform of his wheelchair. "God almighty, Tommy, smells like something's dead in here. Thought you was gonna wash while I was out."

"I like when you do it." He tucked the binoculars under his arm.

"Well, you can just forget that." Eyes closed tight, she wet a sponge at the sink and slid it around her face and neck. "Thought Swainsboro was hot in August," she said, tossing the sponge into the sink, "but this damn Atlanta, I mean to tell ya." Flip-flops slapped on her slow shuffle to the window. "Get yourself all worked up again watching that whore?"

"Saw her the one time, Barbara Jean," he said. "Sorry I even told you."

"If you think I'm putting out the fire she started, you are slap-dead wrong. I gotta get to work." Dropping into a crouch, she hopped like a frog after the runaway soup cans. Along with another flash of tattoo, a bit of stomach squeezed from under her bare-midriff top, hiding her belt buckle.

Frowning, he wiggled a finger at her. "Should you be wearing stuff like that anymore?"

She stood, cradled the cans under her small breasts, and scanned the windows across the street. "What stuff?"

"I dunno. Don't need to be advertising the goods any more is what I'm saying."

Hip-throwing steps brought her next to him. "I'm eighteen. This is how we dress. Don't like it? Tough shit." She pinched at the shoulder of his Harley Davidson tee-shirt. "Where'd this come from?"

"Beau brought it yesterday. Pretty awesome, huh?"

"Damn near kill your fool self on a bike, and that jerkoff brings this?"

"Barbara Jean," he said, raising an open hand, "lay off Beau. Tired of telling you."

She shook her head. "Perfect for each other, you two. Couple of brain-dead scarecrows."

He laughed. "Maybe so." One hand brought the glasses back to his eyes. The other slipped between her legs from behind, clamping her thigh to the side of the wheelchair. He dropped the binoculars onto his chest. "Now that we got *that* over with." His open hand pumped a foot above his lap. "Think you might go get that sponge?"

"*Knew* this was coming," she said, twisting her hips. "Told you. I gotta get ready for work."

"Won't take long. I guarantee it." His free hand undid the top of his cutoff jeans. "C'mon now, BJ," he said, grinning at her.

"You promised to stop calling me that." She nodded toward the window. "And that slut's the one got you like this. Get her to do you."

"Hush now." Both his arms rocked her leg, swaying her hips. "C'mon now. Nothing wrong with a poor cripple asking his wife for a relaxing afternoon." He loosened his grip. "How about you free up them hands, too," he said, raising his chin at the cans.

She scanned the room, closed her eyes, and shook her head.

"Careful!" he said as soup cans bombed onto his lap.

Shade down, she positioned herself in front of him in the semi-dark. "Don't touch me, and don't talk."

THUMPS ON THE APARTMENT DOOR woke him. The doorknob rattled. "Tommy, it's me. Open up."

"Hang on, Beau." He lolled his head, rubbed sleep-stiffness out of his neck.

"Dude, let's go," Beau said, banging harder. "Smells like someone pissed on a fire out here."

He turned the deadbolt and wheeled back from the door.

Beau angled his face around the edge, eased inside, and clicked the lock behind him. A quick glance around the apartment ended with his eyes fixed on the bedroom door. "Ever take those binoculars off, Tommy Boy?"

"She picked up some lunch shifts, superman. You're safe."

"You're an asshole. Y'know that? She doesn't scare me." Beau breezed past him to the open window. "Get your morning show today, horn dog?"

"You're talking to a hunter, son. What do you think?"

"That is one fine specimen." Peering at the windows across the street, Beau reached backwards. "Gimme."

"She's dressed and gone. Been watching other stuff for almost an hour."

"Awesome. Any got tits like her?"

Tommy laughed. "Nothing like that. Been looking at clouds, folks at the bus stop, things like that. Do it most of the day."

"See," Beau said, shaking his head, "life isn't fair. Here I am, stuck at college, drinking beer, snagging pussy, and you get to watch people at a bus stop all day. Just not right."

"Kinda fun, actually. Try to figure out who they are, where they're going. Y'know."

"Want me to kill you?" Beau poked his chin at the rifle case propped in the corner. "Peg one through your head right now if you want."

"I'll let you know."

Beau sat on the sill and pointed to the cast. "Speaking of killing, gonna be hunting season right after you're out of that thing. Make sure your Uncle Wendell knows you, me, and Deacon are coming again this year."

"Yeah, well. We'll have to see."

"What's that mean?"

"Have to talk to Barbara Jean first," he said, turning his gaze out the window.

"You nuts? Isn't gonna be a Barbara Jean."

He shifted in the wheelchair, flipped his eyes between Beau and the toes sticking out of his cast. "Been thinking. May just, y'know, hang around awhile longer."

"You gotta be shittin' me." Beau rocked onto his feet. "Something happen I don't know about? She knocked up for sure this time?"

"No, there ain't no baby."

"Then you're still free, dude. Stick to the plan. Soon as you're walking, your first steps are out that door."

"To go where? Back to Swainsboro? Live with my momma? Stock shelves at the Family Dollar?" He wrinkled his nose, shook his head.

"Stay here in Atlanta with me and Deacon. Live in the dorm with us. Nobody'd care."

"She's sticking by me, Beau. Lost the baby. Had to quit school and get a job because of the accident, but she's still here. And it ain't easy what she has to do."

Beau paced a two-step line, head shaking. "Who the hell I been listening to for the past three months, going on and on about how she trapped you with that baby?" He stopped and leaned in. "Wasn't that you? Sure as hell looked like you?"

"I never said that. You did. Maybe I just never said you was wrong."

"No difference in my mind. And when she said she lost it, wasn't it you who said you were free to leave now, and that's what you were going to do? At least until that old bastard laid your bike over."

"I owe her. People can change, Beau."

"Dude, you're losing your mind in this dump. We're not talking about your momma. This is the girl on the Internet."

41

He gripped the wheels and rolled a few inches toward Beau. "That was before. She's a wife now. *My* wife."

Hands raised, Beau turned his back and wandered to the window.

"I think maybe we could be a family, Beau."

"You and her." Beau glanced back over his shoulder. "A family."

He nodded.

"They change your medication since yesterday?"

"How about we change the subject? Talk about your bike or something."

Beau moseyed to the table. He spun a chair backwards and flopped onto the plastic seat. "What about you?" he said, his arms hanging over the backrest. "You gonna ride again once you're healed?"

"On what, butthead? Got hardly nothing from the insurance, and Barbara Jean's kinda tight with the bucks." He shook his head. "You know we ain't even got a phone, so there sure as hell ain't no Harley in the budget."

"Keep telling you, jackass, get a free one from the damn government."

"And I keep telling you. If I can't afford it, I don't want it."

"Can't tell sometimes if you're stubborn or just plain stupid. And 'budget', for crissake." Beau covered his face. "That's a damn joke. Nineteen-year-olds don't have budgets." He gripped the back of the chair and leaned a grin toward Tommy. "Know what else is kinda funny? The way it's 'Barbara Jean' all the time now. No more BJ." He snorted. "If there was ever someone born to a name."

"Shut up, Beau."

"She winked every time she said her name, for crissake."

Tommy covered his ears. "Don't do this."

"Every day you stay with her is one less happy day in your life," Beau said, stabbing a finger, "and you know it."

He turned his face to the window. "Don't come 'round no more."

Beau flinched. "What're you talking about? This is me, Tommy."

"No. It's different now, but you won't listen."

"Bullshit. You need someone to wipe your ass, so all of a sudden she's a wife, instead of a porn—" Beau's eyes flicked at him.

"Are you retarded?"

"C'mon," Beau said, jumping to his feet, "let's get you out of here before it's too late. Pack your shit. Right now. We'll leave her a note and take the hell off."

"Listen for once. You gotta let people have a fresh start." He slapped both palms on the armrests of the wheelchair. "Got six more weeks in this thing, and I'm gonna use them to give her a chance." He folded his arms. "And I see how it's gonna be. You're the one making me choose, and I'm choosing my wife." He shifted in the seat. "I ain't kidding. Don't come here no more."

Beau snapped a kick into the chair and sent it tumbling across the room. He stomped to the door but didn't open it. "Tommy," he said, without turning, "I never told you this because I don't know for sure if she's right, or if she just doesn't like BJ, which I know she doesn't. When I told my sister Marlene that BJ lost the baby, she laughed. Said BJ was never pregnant. And then she—"

"Bull. How could she know that?"

"Her tits. They never got bigger like they should've. Marlene said BJ was just getting fatter 'cause she's a prize cow, and you're a total fool, falling for such an old trick. She said BJ's been bent over every tailgate in Emanuel County, but picked you as the daddy because you're the idiot, martyr type. Easy pickins for a sneaky bitch wanting to get away from a bad life."

"And that's Marlene talking?"

"My hand to God."

"Well, don't much matter now. What is, is." He rubbed his face with both hands. "Sorry, Beau. Take care of yourself."

"Tommy, don't be too prideful when this blows up. You know where to find me." The door clicked shut without Beau ever looking back into the room.

SHUFFLING FEET AND WHEEZY BREATHS got louder in the hall. Whoever was out there stopped in front of their apartment door. At the first knock, Tommy popped his wheelchair away from the window and blocked Barbara Jean's path from the sink. "I got it," he said.

Dressed in her waitress uniform, she dried her hands on the company apron and drifted along beside him. "If it's that piece of shit, Beau," she said, "don't even think of asking him in here." Gaze trained on the door, she smoothed her hands over her hair and across her backside. "I won't have him in my place."

"It ain't Beau."

More knocks.

"And this is *my* place, too," he said in a rough whisper,

finger poking at her face. "Y'aint telling me who my friends are gonna be. Not now. Not ever."

A third round of raps, stronger this time. "Please open up," a man said. "I can hear you talking in there."

He rolled toward the door

"Hey, moron," she whispered, "gimme them binoculars." Her finger swung toward the window. "Might be that whore's boyfriend or daddy, comin' over here to knock your damn teeth out."

A quick peek at the knob and he lifted the strap over his head and handed them to her.

She shuffled into the bedroom.

Finishing the glide to the door, he opened it to a fat man with shaggy gray hair. Had on a light gray suit with dark circles under the arms. The man held a briefcase in one hand and a business card in the other. "Do you know your elevator's out of order?" he said.

Tommy smiled. "You come up four flights to tell me that?"

The man set his briefcase on the cracked tiles in the hallway and snaked a large handkerchief from his inside breast pocket. He dabbed his face and flabby neck before stuffing the soggy rag back in his pocket. A puzzled look grew on his face. "Don't you remember me, Mr. Pickett?"

"Should I?"

Inching his feet closer to the inside of the apartment, the man pushed the business card at him. "I visited your hospital room. Remember now? Ansel Baldridge, Attorney at Law?"

Hands clasped in his lap, Tommy bounced his chin

at the card. "Got more than a dozen when I was in there. Didn't keep one of them. Got no use for lawyers."

Smiling, Mr. Baldridge fanned the card. "Then I'd be correct in assuming you're not already represented by counsel in the matter of your devastating traffic accident?"

"If you mean have I got a lawyer, no." His glance dropped to the man's knees, now touching the cast. "And I don't want one," he said, his gaze rising to the man's face. "The old guy's insurance company's taking good care of me. Paying the medical bills and such."

The attorney tipped his head back and laughed. "Ah, would that we were all so innocent." He shook the card again. "Please, may I come in? I'm going to make you a very wealthy man, Mr. Pickett. Ah," he said, his eyes shifting to something behind Tommy, "and if this lovely woman is your wife, my timing couldn't be better. This involves her as well."

"Let Mr. Baldridge pass, Tommy."

He gawked at his wife's hand, stuck out for a handshake.

"Barbara Jean Pickett," she said. "Couldn't help but hear, place being small like it is." She backed into the room. "Have a seat," she said, pointing to a chair at the card table. Her nose crinkled as she sat. "We ain't got much. Just starting out."

Big smile on his face, the lawyer dropped into a chair and swung his briefcase onto the table. "Well, Mrs. Pickett, it's going to take a little time, but I can assure you that the injuries your husband suffered, combined with the burdens they've placed upon you, are going to make your futures supremely more comfortable."

"Sir, you're wasting your time," Tommy said, joining

them at the table. "Already told you, got no use for lawyers. That old man didn't whack into me on purpose. Leave him be."

"*Jails* are for people who do things on purpose, Mr. Pickett. Civil courts and insurance exist to help repair the shattered lives of innocent victims like yourselves." He squinted inside his overstuffed case and pulled out a manila folder. "And," he said, tapping a finger on the folder, "eighty-three-year-old Dr. Conrad Fletcher of Buckhead *and* Lake Oconee, Georgia, carries a delightful amount of it." He loosened his tie and mopped his face with the handkerchief he'd fished from his jacket. "Good lord, no air conditioning? How do you stand this? Mrs. Pickett, may I trouble you for some water."

"Where are my manners?" She sprang from the table. "Some fine waitress I am."

"In the interests of my survival," the lawyer said toward the sink, "is there another way for us to discuss this without my having to climb up here?"

"Call my cell," she said over the rush of the running water. "Number's—" She shot a glance at Tommy and giggled. "Where's my head at? I meant my job. You can call me at my job at TGI—"

"Hold it," Tommy said. "You got a phone, Barbara Jean?"

The lawyer leaned over a yellow pad, ballpoint at the ready. "Sorry, Mrs. Pickett, I missed that."

"Excuse me, sir." Tommy pushed the pen flat onto the paper and held it there. "Barbara Jean, I asked you a question."

Eyebrows raised, she placed a glass of water in front

of the lawyer. "This ain't the time, honey. Now let Mr. Baldridge finish his business."

Tommy's gaze never left her. He slid the ballpoint from the lawyer's hand and flipped it onto his belly. "Business is finished. I got your card if I ever change my mind. You best be leaving now."

"Perhaps another time would be better. This heat. I'm not feeling very well." The sound of papers being crammed into a briefcase mixed with the lawyer's words. "I'll see myself out." He paused at the open door. "Perhaps one of you could just call when—"

"Get out!" He spun the wheelchair and rushed at Mr. Baldridge's startled face. The lawyer slammed the door and Tommy faced back into the room, blocking the exit.

She stood near the sink, arms folded, chin raised.

"When'd you get a phone?"

"Don't talk to me like that. Like I'm under arrest or something."

"One of them damn government phones?"

"If you must know, my manager, Slade, he give it to me. Says I'm his best girl, and any extra shifts that open up can be mine, but he's gotta to be able to reach me. And he's paying, so what do you care for?"

"Give it here," he said, reaching an open hand toward her.

She shifted her weight to the other foot and stared at him.

"Girl, you plan on getting outta here, you best give me that phone."

Her face went blank. She backed to the kitchen counter and felt for her purse. After some clunks inside it, her hand came out holding the phone. She took small steps toward him and let out a squeaky giggle. "For all the good it'll do you. Like giving a fiddle to a snake. Here." She underhanded it from about five feet and backed behind the card table.

"Think I'm some kinda idiot, do you?" He powered up the phone after a single glance. "Uncle Wendell brings a damn satellite phone when we go hunting. Half the kids in school had phones, for godsake. I seen and used plenty of these." He worked some keys. "So, let's see who you been talking to."

"This is stupid. Y'ain't gonna know them numbers. Give it here."

"This one ends in 00. That's probably the restaurant. And this one's your momma. Damn witch didn't even show up at the wedding. Why you talking to her?" He tilted his head and wiggled the phone at her. "Who's 6642? Lots of those."

"I ain't putting up with this." She held out her hand, but stayed behind the table. "I want my phone back. Now."

He checked the screen again. "How about we just highlight one, push 'send,' and see who picks up." He pressed the phone to his ear, settled back, and smiled.

"You got no right," she said, dashing around the table.

Stiff-arms and roll-aways held her off. He switched the phone to his far away hand every time she circled the wheelchair.

The sound of ringing got her more frantic. "Slade, don't!" She bounced fists and slaps off Tommy's head and shoulders.

"Hi, baby," a man's voice said.

Hand clamped over the mouthpiece, Tommy hunched forward and pressed the speaker against his ear.

"Coming over?" the man said.

"Here." He shoved it through her flapping arms and twisted it into her chin.

She snatched it with two hands and rocked onto her heels. "Call you later," she said into the phone and hung up. Shuffling backward toward her purse, she tapped fingertips to her chin and checked them. "Have you arrested. Damn moron."

"How long?"

The phone vibrated in her hand. She turned it off and set it on the counter.

"I asked you a question."

"Y'know, I'm glad really." She covered her eyes and let out a long breath. "Tommy, you got every right to be mad, but I want you to know, this ain't just a fooling around thing. I'm in love with Slade." Her eyes met his. "I'm sorry. I really am."

Unblinking, he let his head roll side to side.

"Well?" she said, eyes wide. "Gonna say something?"

"Were you pregnant?"

"Idiot," she whispered. "What's that got to do with now?" Head shaking, she took a step toward her purse. "Look, I know we need to talk, but I gotta go to work. We'll sort this out later."

A snake-strike of the wheelchair spooked her into a corner.

"What are you doing?" she said.

"Answer my question."

"Said I'm sorry." Her eyes darted around the room.

"Anything more would only be hurtful. Where's the good in that? C'mon now. Let me by." She moved to get around him.

"No!" He spun the cast into her leg, making it buckle.

"God *dammit.*" Pain on her face, she grabbed above her knee. "Alright," she said, teeth bared. "Alright, big man, you wanna do this? Let's do it." Wedged between the two walls, she leaned forward and shimmied her shoulders. "So, what do you really wanna know? Boy like you who just *loves* his binoculars must want lots of details. Wanna know where we do it? How often? What positions? Is he better'n you? Bigger'n you? Spit or— No, y'already know that one." Finger pressed to her cheek, she swept her eyes across the ceiling. "Let's see, I miss anything?"

"Were you pregnant?"

"Jesus H. *Christ!*" she said, fists tapping against her temples. "Like talking to Forest Gump."

"Listen good, BJ," he said, pushing tall in the chair. "I'm serious now. You listening?"

She glared and rubbed her leg.

"I already know the answer, but you're gonna tell me. And here's the important part." He raised one finger. "You don't tell me the truth? First time? You're leaving here with a sheet over your face."

Her big eyes danced between him and the door. "Alright," she said, shoulders sagging, "I wasn't. But I swear, I didn't know that when I told you. I was three days late. Never was late before, so I figured, y'know, I was that way."

"I ain't stupid. There was others. Why me?"

She winced and massaged her leg. "Dammit, this really hurts. What'd you do that for?"

He backed away and bobbed his head toward the

fridge. "Probably should put some ice on it. And answer my question," he said as she limped by.

"I dunno. Always something decent about you. Quiet, serious. Figured you'd stand up if need be." Smiling, she dumped ice cubes onto a dishtowel. "And then you was so sweet to me about the baby. Guess I didn't want that to stop. Next I knew, I was at my own damn wedding. Shocked the hell outta me to wake up as Mrs. Pickett, I promise you."

"Why'd you stay?"

"Where was I gonna go?" She groaned with each step. "And then good things started to happen. I got into beauty school down here. You got the job at the dealership. Thought maybe being married was lucky or something. Then you wiped out, and that was that."

"I'm gonna be fine again. You couldn't wait?"

She sat and rested the ice bag on her leg. "Why we talking about this? Ain't like we love each other. Or ever did. Not ready to be a wife. Yours or anybody's. And tending to you taught me I'm sure as hell in no hurry to be a momma."

"When you going?"

She shrugged. "Thought this was gonna happen after you was on your feet." Her nose crinkled. "Y'know, I could still stay until then if you want. Feel like I owe you something. He don't have to know you found out."

"What about the phone thing just now?"

"I'll figure something." She peeked under the towel, then at him. "So, you want me to?"

"Just leave me the phone," he said, head shaking slowly. "I'll take it from there."

"Ain't mine to give."

A laugh burst out of his mouth.

Her gaze dropped to the floor next to him. "I say something funny?"

"Can you go to this guy tonight? For good, I mean?"

"Pretty sure."

"Leave the phone with me. When you come for your stuff tomorrow, it'll be on the table. I won't be here."

She looked from him, to her phone, then back. "I suppose." Gimpy steps took her toward the counter. "Where you gonna go?"

"That don't concern you."

She tossed the towel in the sink and continued to the counter and her purse. "Catch," she said, flipping the phone to him. Shuffling steps brought her next to his cast. "Guess this is it then." Both her hands stroked the plaster. "You gonna divorce me? Or do I do it?"

"Me."

"Okay." She backed toward the bedroom and tapped a finger to the side of her chin. "Gonna put makeup on this and get some clothes for tonight."

Only a minute or two passed before she came out carrying a stuffed tote bag. "Just want you to know," she said, her hand on the knob, "I'm suing that old man for busting you up. Mr. Baldridge says I can, even if you won't."

"Oh, man." His head flopped against the back of the chair. "I really am a moron. Was you who called him."

"Slade, actually. Said it'd be stupid not to. I forget what he called it, but I get money because we couldn't screw. You and me, that is." She shrugged and smiled. "Kinda funny if you think about it."

He stared at her.

"Maybe not," she said. "Well, take care of yourself, Tommy. Hope things work out good for you, too."

Once he couldn't hear her steps in the hall or the stairwell anymore, he rolled into bedroom. Through the open closet door, he noticed the binoculars tucked at the back of the top shelf.

"*Damn* her."

He scooted back into the other room, stripped the case off his rifle, and snapped on the scope. Parked alongside the window, he laid the barrel on the sill and rolled the adjustment wheel. Blurry turned to clear as she crossed the street to the bus stop, off on the first day of a new life. Her head drifted in and out of the cross-hairs, and then she paused.

"Blam." Puff of steam from her hair. Forward lurch. Burst of wet red onto the sidewalk.

He continued to track her.

She hopped onto the curb.

"Blam." Bullseye into the tramp stamp dropped her to her knees. Face-first pitch onto the bench.

Bag of clothes at her ankles, she sat, spread her arms on the top slat, and yawned.

"Blam." A shot exploded into her gaping mouth.

The gun sight dropped to her belly. One eye watched the soft swell rise and fall until a bus showed up and blocked his view. He watched until it left, but she was gone.

MOVING HOME

HERE HE COMES, the pig-faced runt. Weaving through the tables. Hands waving over his head. Capped teeth gleaming in that punch-inviting smile.

"Hey-hey, Travis Rutledge," he calls from about thirty feet away. "Been a while."

The bullshit, full name shout-out. He only does it so I have to yell it back, catch any agent or casting director in earshot. "Glen Carletto," I say, rising to my feet. "Great to see you, man." Have to stoop for the thumb-grip, chest bump, and shoulder slap. "So, how's life at the top?"

"Cappuccino, half-caf," Glen says to the approaching waiter. He grins and sits. "The top? Got the wrong boy, dude." He unrolls his setup, snaps the napkin, spreads it on his lap. His face tips skyward. "Is this a day or what?"

It's December, but warm enough for an outside table at *Dreams* on Sunset. The humming lunchtime crowd is shirt-sleeved and bare-legged, sucking up the unobstructed SoCal sun. Empowering, blinding. Three-hundred-dollar sunglasses sit on every rhinoplasty. Coconut sunscreen mixes with mesquite-grilled entrees and fried sides. The delicious smells are making me insane. "Gotta give you credit, Glen," I tell him. "You never slip on my name."

"Not that tough, really. You look way more like a Travis Rutledge than a Malcolm Spong." He wobbles his head and blinks fast. "I mean, holy shit. First time we met in New York I told you that name was toxic. Remember? Said it sounds like gettin' a hard-on." His fist pops up from the table. "Sponnnng."

"You've done that one to death. Okay?"

He shrugs and sits forward, bites his lower lip, rat-a-tats fingers against the edge of the table. "So, what's so secret and important you couldn't tell me on the phone? If you're up for something good," his thumb pumps at his chest, "don't forget to mention your friends."

"I'm finished, Glen."

"Ah, Christ, again?"

"I need money to go back east. Figured it would be harder for you to say no if we were face to face."

He tips his chair onto the back legs, drags fingers into his shiny black waves. His face crumples. "We been through this, like what, three months ago?"

"I didn't ask for money then. Now I need it."

"So get a waiter job. Do some substitute teaching. Save up for a few months, then go. Don't do this to me, man." He swivels his head side to side, looks at anything but my face.

"I can't. None of that stuff. My car got repossessed. Yesterday." I lean closer. "Don't make me go through this shit. We go back a long way. Just front me five hundred and wish me luck. And don't tell me you don't have it."

"Dude, I made nine grand out here in six years. How do you figure I have five hundred for you?"

My head is shaking the whole time he's talking. "This is me, Glen. When we were trying off-Broadway, you were the unemployed guy with his own apartment, nice clothes, the right haircut. All of it." I tap a finger on my front teeth. "Even these. Your Wall Street family's floated you since I've known you. Play poverty for a different audience."

He knits his fingers together, stares at them like I'm not even there.

I stretch across the table, grab his wrists, and pull his hands apart. "Would I ask if I wasn't desperate? And did you even hear me, douche bag? They repossessed my car. No way I can work in L.A. without a car."

"Take cabs." He tugs his hands free and backs away. "Or get a job near home."

His cappuccino arrives. We stop talking until the waiter/actor/screenwriter leaves. Glen frowns into the oversized cup as he stirs in three packets of Splenda, one after the other.

Getting nowhere here. My hands ball into fists under the table. Looks like he's going to have to hear the worst part. I only want to say it once, so the words have to come out slow and clear. "Glen, I have no home anymore. I was living in my car. Just dumb luck I was there when the guy hooked it, or I wouldn't even have my stuff anymore."

His face goes blank. "What?" Lips still apart, he tips his head forward and peers over the top of his wraparound Oakleys. "You mean like … living?"

"Living."

He goes back to stirring his cappuccino again, scraping and dinging the spoon. Each ping hits like my head's inside a cathedral bell. I want to sweep the cup off the table, watch it explode on the stone terrace. He lifts it with two hands and blows on the whipped cream. As if that's doing anything. Moron. After a couple of slurps, he peeks at me over the rim. More like a squint. He clatters the china onto the saucer, pinches away a foam mustache, and smacks his lips. "Best cappuccino in the friggin' galaxy." One eye closes about halfway. "How tall are you? Six-five?"

"Little more. Why?"

His eyes widen. "Don't you drive a VW?"

"I do … Did."

"You. In a Volkswagen Beetle."

I lean toward him. "That's what I'm telling you."

He sits back and sweeps a finger at me. "How'd you sleep?"

There's a puzzled look on his face. Could be a smirk. Got this guy by nine inches and sixty pounds. Nothing more I'd like right now than to backhand him into a coma and leave an IOU in his wallet. "You'd be surprised how much room there is when the passenger seat's taken out. More than enough space for a sleeping bag. Pretty comfortable, really."

"What about bathrooms, showers, stuff like that." He's still eyeballing me.

"Friends, girls' apartments now and then, gas stations, dorms at Pepperdine once in a while. Lots of places."

"Sounds terrible."

"You should try it for a while, you trust fund piece o' shit."

He doesn't smile.

"Lighten up. I'm kidding. But to be honest, there's something, I dunno, liberating about it. I kinda understand why the homeless don't want to go to shelters. Life on my own terms. Rain and cold weren't a problem, and I liked waking up wherever I wanted. Felt like an adventure most of the time."

"And now?"

I'm not telling him I woke up sitting on a toilet at the bus station this morning, everything I own — sleeping bag, small suitcase, and a garbage bag of clothes — in the stall with me. "And now the adventure's over. All of it. So I'm asking an old friend for a little temporary help."

"Thought you were doing okay?" He's clinking that goddam spoon again, flicking his eyes between me and the cappuccino. "All those commercials you did. They had to pay good. What happened?"

"Are you really in this business nine years?"

He frowns at me. "What's that supposed to mean?"

"It means you should know what happened. I'd give my portfolio to casting directors, and they'd barely open it. 'Oh yeah, the Noxzema guy. That was nice work,' or, 'So that's where I know you. You're the Albertson's guy.' Then they'd shove it back and say something like, 'I don't see you for this part.' I haven't done anything but dinner theatre for over two years. And I only made big money on Noxzema because it was nationwide. That was four years ago."

He doesn't say anything, just keeps eyeing me. I flop back in the seat, trying not to look angry. "Glen, my financial history is pointless bullshit. I'm tapped. Whatever I made is gone. And I haven't even read for anything in months, so nothing's coming up. Five hundred gets me back to New York. I'll send it to you in a couple weeks. A month, tops. How about it?"

"Wow. Noxzema was four years ago?" The words

are soft, distant. His eyes wander, then land on me again. "How old are you now?"

"Thirty-one." My chest gets light. It's like someone else said it. Sounds like a number that should have some life-in-motion stuff behind it.

"That's still plenty young. Hell, I'm thirty-three." He shakes his head. "And why the hell you want to go east in December? You'll freeze to death after living out here so long. At least wait until spring. And I wouldn't even go then. There's *way* more work out here. Who knows? Maybe something'll come up." His eyes run up and down at me. "You got that John Wayne/Clint Eastwood thing going. Maybe that'll be big again." He gets this look like he's in pain. "You can't just quit. Real actors don't quit."

"This one did." I need to go for the close again. "Please, Glen. I need the five hundred, and I need it today. You'll get it back. I swear."

"Sorry, man. I don't have it." He shakes his head, bunches his lips to the side of his face, and stares at me.

"How about three hundred? That's enough for me to take the bus." Found that out this morning while I was strolling around the bus station, playing a frustrated traveler.

"No hundreds, dude. I got *nada*." Another noisy sip of his cappuccino. "Have you talked to your folks?"

"They turned me down." He doesn't have to know I haven't called them. "Said I'm a man now. Pay my own way. Tough love, I guess."

He shakes his head again. "Shit, that's cold."

We both lean back, say nothing, look at each other, don't look at each other.

"Okay. No problem." I push away from the table and stand. "Gotta take a squirt. If the waiter comes by, order me a refill, will you? Diet Coke."

"Actually, I gotta get going." He checks his phone and starts to get up.

My hand on his shoulder pins him in the seat. "Hang for two seconds. I'm gonna kill some more time here, and I don't want to lose the table. I'll be right back."

"Just hurry, okay?" He rolls his eyes. "I'm already late."

After using the facilities, I stroll out the front door, past the terrace where he's slouched in the chair, flipping his goddam bell-clapper spoon. I walk backwards down the sidewalk, wave my arms over my head. "Glen Carletto," I yell, big smile on my face.

He snaps upright in the chair.

"Thanks for the drink. Lunch'll be on me next—"

His spoon helicopters past my face and clangs off the door of a black 911 Carrera. Makes a ding in the paint shaped like a fingernail clipping.

"That's my car, asshole!" some guy shouts. Glen sinks into the chair as the guy stomps to his table. He's going to be down more than five hundred just touching up the nick in the paint. Good. Lying scumbag.

Got no place to go, other than the bus station. The thought of rejoining that hygiene-challenged collection of bottom feeders doesn't thrill me, but my things are in a locker. I'm anxious that one of them will figure a way to break in before I work this thing out. That stuff's all I have right now. I want to see it, touch it.

The fact that it's almost an hour's walk doesn't bother me, until I get dizzy after about ten minutes. Haven't eaten since yesterday lunch, and someone my size burns through a ninety-nine cent burrito pretty fast. A bus stop bench keeps me from having to sit on the curb while the fuzziness passes. I rest my forearms on my thighs and hang my head between my knees. Could kick myself for not sticking Glen with a big meal.

Popping lights begin to fade. Focus gets clear enough to start creating the script I'll recite to whichever parent accepts the call. Don't want to ad lib, so I improv the scene out loud, right there at the side of the road. Thumb touching my ear, I talk into my pinky. "Mom? Dad? Let me start by telling you I'm okay. My car was totaled in an accident yesterday. Yeah, hit and run. Like I said, I'm pretty much okay, except for a sprained back. I'm having a little trouble walking, but they tell me it'll pass in a month or so."

Sounds pretty good, so I stand to practice my limp, work on some more dialogue.

"Since this is going to keep me from working for a while, what I'd like to do is come home and convalesce with you guys. With it being Christmas and all, it's a perfect time. My only problem is, of course, I didn't foresee this possibility. I haven't put away enough to get another car, keep paying my rent, *and* pay for the airfare home. So if you can swing it, would you please buy the ticket? One way is fine. I'll pay my way back here."

No caring parent could turn that down. I hobble down the street and look for a pay phone. Takes forever to find one that isn't busted. I pick up the receiver, but put it back. Not ready yet. Some jigging and facial exercises, a little head-rolling. The stuff I always do before going on. Okay. Big breath. Action.

The operator comes on. "Collect call from Malcolm," I tell him and wait for someone to pick up in Old Tappan, New York.

My father says he'll accept the charges. "Malcolm, huh?" he shouts, like he's gone a little deaf since last time. "Haven't called yourself that in a while. What happened to Travis?"

"Dad," is all I can get out. I see my old room and the bed I was too big for by tenth grade. T&A posters. Little League trophies. A fat PC monitor on the junior desk. "Dad," I choke out one more time as my gaze drifts up to the bleary sky.

THE SIN IN THE CEMETERY

"MANLEY, RATS!"

Scorza's annoying voice knocked Manley out of a comfortable, hot-day haze. Staying on his back under the ancient maple, he lifted the baseball hat covering his face and looked up.

Ten feet above, Scorza dangled from a branch by one hand. The other held his buttered Kaiser roll. He shook the snack toward Section B. "Two of them. They going to that new grave?"

"How the hell would I know, Monkey Boy?" he said, pushing to his feet.

"Keep calling me that, douche bag," Scorza said, "and I swear to God, you're gonna wake up dead. Don't care how big you are."

The third grass cutter, Sullivan, hopped onto a nearby pipe railing. He teetered and scanned where Scorza had pointed.

Manley joined him. "I don't see anything, Monkey Boy." He shielded his eyes. "Where?"

Without answering, Scorza dropped to the ground and took off on a steeplechase, vaulting and hurdling through a maze of gravebeds, trees, headstones, and railings.

Knees flexed, Sullivan looked like he was about to join the hunt.

"Take it easy, College Boy," Manley said, gripping the back of Sullivan's denim shirt. "That grave's not going anywhere." He stepped off the rail, dragging the gangly Sullivan with him like a life-sized ventriloquist's dummy. "If it's a cheap casket, they'll be busy for a while. Relax." He let go of the shirt and offered a cigarette from the pack he'd unrolled from the sleeve of his t-shirt.

"I'm a runner." Sullivan's face twisted like he was smelling raw sewage.

"Oh, yeah." He tucked the cigarette over his ear and started walking in Scorza's direction. "Big time athlete. Scholarship."

"Partial," Sullivan said from half a stride behind, "and I'm not actually 'College Boy' until September."

They dropped into single file on a bluestone path through the Braverman family plot.

"Manley, why do you keep calling Scorza 'Monkey Boy'? He really hates it."

Without turning, he popped a finger into the air. "One, he looks like a monkey." A second finger. "Two, who the hell climbs a tree every time he eats something?" Third finger. "And mostly, because he hates it. Kinda fun watching his routine." He bounced from boot to boot. "I'll kill you, Manley," he said in a screechy falsetto, "I'll kill your mother. I'll kill your fuckin' dog."

"That's a pretty good Scorza," Sullivan said, chuckling.

Manley stopped in front of a small family plot. He rolled the cigarette off his ear and lit it. "Hey," he said, pointing to *Sarah Kontoff's* headstone, "know what her husband's name was? Fokker." The smoking match bounced off a cracked porcelain photograph of the woman.

Sullivan pointed to the stone next to hers. "This says David."

"What a tool." Manley shook his head and headed down the path.

"How long is this going to take?" Sullivan said as they got back onto the main road. "Break's only ten minutes. Won't Jake be making rounds pretty soon?"

"That lard-ass mutant won't come out in this heat. Told you, relax."

Birds whistled and twittered. Cicadas whirred. Boots clomped to the rhythm of Sullivan's slapping arm, one whack to the leg for every second stride.

"Something bugging you, College Boy?"

"A little, I guess. How come Jews don't, y'know, embalm?"

"Jesus Christ," Manley said, tenting a hand over his eyes. "Where do you come up with these?"

"Wouldn't that stop the rats?"

"This way." He flicked Sullivan's shoulder and hopped over a railing of the Beth Shalom Burial Society. "So that's it. Rats. You afraid?"

"Wouldn't say afraid," Sullivan said, loping to catch up. "Not my favorite mammal. I'll give you that."

"Thought they were rodents."

"Rodents are mammals."

"Oh, 'Rodents *are* mammals'. Look at me, the genius." he said in a nasally voice. "Doesn't matter. You're afraid."

"Go screw yourself, Manley." A few more strides and

the leg slapping started again. "Cremation would work for sure. Why don't they do that?"

"Y'know, pointless crap like this is what made me quit school."

"C'mon, you're the one who told me visitors leave pebbles on the headstones as a sign of respect, so I know you know stuff."

Manley slumped at the knees and shoulders but kept going. "Just not allowed. Okay? Must be a sin, or a sacrilege, or something."

"Whose sin? The dead person can't be blamed, and why would God care anyway? The soul's the important part, and that's already gone."

"Sullivan. That's Irish. Catholic, right?"

"So? What're you?"

He picked a pebble off *Saul Meyerowitz*, grunted as he whizzed it past a small clay pot resting on *David Silverman*. "Nothing."

"Well, that doesn't mean you can't think about stuff. Like, what about this? Rats are part of creation, too. You think God might *want* them to eat the bodies?"

"You're an idiot. How the hell could anyone know that? Like being with a five-year-old. Daddy, how high is up?"

Sullivan stopped. "I like to understand things. What's wrong with that? This place is like outer space to me, and you're here the longest. Why wouldn't I ask you?"

Noisy exhales rushed through his nose as he squinted at Sullivan. "Alright. Pretty sure their book says if they die before noon, they have to be planted the same day. If it's after noon, then it's the next morning. Either way, a body's gotta be buried. In three years, I never seen an urn in this dump." He spread his arms and started walking again. "Happy, College Boy?"

Sullivan took a step and stopped again. "And this College Boy stuff. Is that because I'm some out of place Poindexter? Or is it a half-assed congratulations for trying to improve my life?"

"You figure it out." He detoured to a nearby gravebed and fished through clumps of earth. Grinning, he hefted one about baseball size and nodded up the road at Scorza who was sitting on top of a chest-high tombstone.

"Tell me something," Sullivan said as they headed toward Scorza. "How many girls you met here in the last three years?"

"What?" He stopped, jaw hanging.

"When you go to a club or a bar, or wherever you spend your paycheck, what do you tell them you do? The girls, I mean. Ever thought about what you're gonna tell them in five years? Ten years?"

He stared and chewed his lips, floated the dirt bomb from hand to hand. On one of the catches, he cocked his arm, then whirled and side-armed it. "Heads up, Monkey Boy."

The grenade burst inches below Scorza's butt, washing sandy clay up his back. He shook the grit from his shirt and hair and twisted toward them. A smile stretched above and below his braces. "They went in there," he said, pointing backwards. "Small hole in the corner. Don't know how many's down there, but I saw four." He turned and locked his eyes onto the grave. "Manley, they're eating that dead Jew, aren't they?"

Bent onto the same monument, Manley rested his chin on his forearms and stared at the mounded earth twenty feet away. "I guess. Seen 'em come and go for days."

"Oh, man." Scorza snapped his fingers. "Be right back." He launched into the air with a pop of his legs. Even before reaching the ground, his feet were running back to where they'd left their mowers.

Sullivan jumped onto the vacancy Scorza left on *Sarah Kleinerman*.

At the new grave Manley read a paper card on the temporary marker. "Tovah Finkelstein, seventy-six." Smile on his face, he jogged back to Sullivan and hopped onto *Harriet Warshafsky*. "Not something I'd consider prime eating material."

"Why are we waiting?" Sullivan said. "Jake's gonna catch us."

"Wanna go? Go."

Hands rubbing on his thighs, Sullivan scanned the area non-stop until he froze. "Someone's coming."

Scorza, grunting and laughing, appeared from behind *Isaac Ishker*. "This is gonna be great." He lowered his spare jug of gasoline to the ground and flexed his fingers. "Goddam thing's a load."

"You're messed up, Monkey Boy. You know that?"

"Bite me. This is gonna be un-fuckin-believable."

Sullivan looked puzzled. "What's going on?"

Excitement lit up Scorza's face. "Gonna give those furry little bastards a taste of hell."

"You gonna let him do this, Manley?"

"Sullivan, go fuck yourself," Scorza said, waddling to the grave, two hands lugging the fuel between his legs.

"Manley," Sullivan's voice grew louder, "this isn't right. It's not just rats down there."

"He ain't my dog," Manley said with a shrug.

Scorza reached the grave and dropped onto all fours. Licking his lips, he guided the spout into the hole.

"That's enough!" Manley jumped from *Harriet Warshafsky* and charged a few steps. He stopped advancing when Scorza scrambled in retreat, dragging the can with him.

"Okay, okay." Scorza glared as he dropped to one knee and slipped a plastic cap on the nozzle. "I already got a mother, Manley. How about you eat shit and die."

Middle finger held high, Manley returned to *Harriet Warshafsky* and ducked behind her. "Guy's nuts. You probably want to get back there," he said, pointing to the rear of *Sarah Kleinerman*.

"You can still stop this. He does what you say."

Manley swallowed away some dryness and crouched behind *Harriet Warshafsky*.

Squatting like a baseball catcher, Scorza lit the scrap of newspaper he'd crammed onto the tip of a branch. Flame touched the soaked hole. The earth shuddered, toppling Scorza onto his back. Flame spurted into the air. Smaller flare-ups slowed until a steady fire burned weakly in the hole.

"Jesus Christ!" Scorza scrambled to his feet. "Jesus Christ!" His arms and legs bounced like a dancing puppet. He raced in ragged circles and figure eights, whooping, laughing, eyes dazzled.

Manley checked all directions as he raced to the snaking column of black smoke. He snatched Scorza by both arms and shook him. "Stop!"

"Manley. Holy *fuck*."

He shook Scorza. "Grab that can and get back to your mower. If Jake shows up, you don't know a thing."

"Again," Scorza said, legs jigging, eyes sparkling. "Wanna do it again."

"Do what I tell you!" A slap cracked against the side of Scorza's head, knocking him onto one hopping leg.

"Hey!" Scorza rubbed above an ear as he backed away. "Who do you think— You're fuckin' dead, pal."

One quick step toward him and Scorza grabbed the can and scurried into the sea of gravestones.

"Kick dirt on the fire," he told a wide-eyed Sullivan. "I'll make sure there's nothing to show we were here."

"Manley," Sullivan said, a hand cupped over his mouth and nose, "smell that? Is that her?"

"Do it!" He shoved Sullivan toward the grave.

Regaining his balance, Sullivan approached the fire from upwind. Small kicks grew to furious side-swipes that heaped waves of earth onto the hole. He got it capped but kept scraping more on top, panting and mumbling.

"Let's go," Manley said, yanking Sullivan away from the grave. He broke into a trot toward their mowers.

Sullivan took a step toward safety but returned to the grave.

"You're on your own, genius."

"I'm coming. It's just …" Sullivan dropped to one knee and made a speedy sign of the cross.

The only words Manley could make out during the mumbled prayer were "Mrs. Finkelstein," "rats," and "sacrilege."

71

Another quick sign of the cross and Sullivan took off in a sprint.

Manley was already jogging, but when Sullivan reached him, the pace clicked up to a jailbreak. "That was … pretty weird …" he said. "You praying … for the rats … like that."

"Y' know," Sullivan said, eyes forward, no trace of effort in his voice, "I think it's too late for you already. You do stuff like that, to that poor woman, but *I'm* weird?" He shook his head, shifted into a new gear, and left him far behind.

"Me?" Manley screamed with his last bit of breath. Feet slapping and arms flailing, he staggered to a stop. A few more steps on jelly-legs and he propped his hands on his knees, gulped breaths in moaning, open-mouthed heaves.

Ahead, Sullivan had reached his mower and was already working.

"Was Scorza," Manley shouted toward the droning machine.

Sullivan sliced a path down an embankment and disappeared.

Hands on his hips, Manley panted through bared teeth while he paced. "Was you, too," he hollered, stabbing a finger in Sullivan's direction. "Why didn't you stop him? Huh? Answer that one, Question Boy." Nodding, he kept poking toward Sullivan. "And that stupid prayer," he shouted through cupped hands. "Think that saved you? Think you're better than everyone? Smarter than everyone?" His body trembled. "Well, you're not!"

Still wobbly, he staggered into some nearby shade, swept a pile of pebbles off *Deborah Weintraub*, and sat. "Oughta go kick his ass." Elbows on his knees, head hanging, he lit a cigarette, but stomped it out after only two drags.

"Son of a *bitch*." He dropped to the ground on all fours and groomed through the grass until *Deborah Weintraub* had her pyramid of pebbles back.

EYES CAN'T LIE

THOMAS PAUSED OUTSIDE the kitchen and blew warm breaths into his hands. He wasn't ready, but he'd never be ready. His wife didn't look up from the pan after his most cheerful, "Morning, Abby." The kiss he pecked on her sunken cheek might as well have been planted on a piece of marble.

"Hi, Daddy," Melanie said from a seat at the kitchen table. Smiling, she offered her cheek to him, globs of pancake showing in her braces. "Know what today is?"

He kissed his daughter and fetched a mug from a cabinet near the stove. "Sorry I was so late," he said in a soft voice as he poured coffee. "I had to drive Cynthia Talbot home."

"As if there's some other Cynthia."

"Daddy, answer me. Know what today is?"

"She had car trouble. What was I supposed to do? No, Melanie," he said, his voice rising to normal as he headed for the table. "Did I forget your birthday?"

"That's in November. You know that. No. Today's like the most awesome day of my life. Jessica's sleepover party. My first ever? Remember now? And omigosh, it's going to be insane." Her hips rocked in the chair.

"Oh yeah. Oh yeah," she chanted, arms flapping like a stork.

A plate of pancakes clunked in front of him. "Thanks," he said to Abby's back. "Aren't you eating?"

"Not hungry."

Still shimmying in her chair, Melanie grinned at him. "Are you two fighting?"

"Braces or not," he said, "lips closed when you eat."

"If you two ever get a divorce, I'm gonna live with Jessica. Then I can have a dog."

He peeked at Abby, her silent attention fixed on the dishes she was rinsing. "Melanie," he said, "what are you talking about?"

"Well, Brittany's parents are getting a divorce. And Renee's parents are divorced. And isn't Mrs. Talbot divorced?"

"Is it twice, Thomas?" Abby said. The skillet sizzled under a spray of tap water. "Or three times?"

He pushed the plate away. "Should have told you sooner, Abby. I don't have time to eat. Have to meet some roofers at the church."

"Thomas." She spun toward him. Her eyes flicked between him and Melanie. "Call me as soon as you're free. It's very important."

He pulled the front door closed, crossed the rectory's covered porch, and trudged down the steps. The cellphone in his pocket vibrated. He loped across the driveway and narrow strip of lawn, sprang up the church's granite steps two at a time. Inside the arched entryway, shielded from any window in the rectory, he dug out his phone. *Cynthia* showed on the Caller I.D. He checked the time. "She's crazy."

At the final hum before voicemail, he pushed *Send.* "Hi," he said, using his back to push open the weighty oak door.

"I didn't sleep at all," she said. "How about you?"

"Not much." Footfalls echoed in the empty church as he headed up the center aisle to the altar. He raked fingers into his hair and left them there. "I know we have to talk, but I've got kind of a nutty morning going here. Roofers are coming any minute. Got my hospital visits after that. Confessions this afternoon. You know, busy. I'll call you soon as I'm done."

"What are we going to do?"

"I'll call you later."

"Wasn't last night magical?"

He nodded, then shook his head. "I'll be done here around four. Call you right after that."

"Come over," she said. "I have this lovely empty house. And I think we've moved beyond passion in the back seat of a Taurus, don't you?"

"Cynthia …" His face burned. "Last night's not going to happen again."

Silence lasted so long he checked the phone's face. "You there?" he said after returning it to his ear.

"So, you're just a talker. Those things you said. All those wonderful things. That was just to get in my pants."

"You know that's not true."

"Unless you mean location," she said after a thin laugh. "I rubbed my knees raw on your upholstery. Had to put makeup on them, for heaven sake."

Squeezing his forehead, he sat on the altar rail, his back to the pews. "We crossed a line. I'm stepping back onto my side. Believe me, I'm sorry."

"Thomas, don't—"

"Stop. This can't go anywhere."

"So, today you don't love me? You were sure last night."

"I should have seen this coming. Done something about it."

"I'm not letting you take it back."

"Cynthia, this is my fault. I know that. I probably should have talked it out with you. Y'know, admit I'm lonely and my feelings for you are dangerous."

"Please, how bloodless. Sounds like Saint Abby."

"Leave her out of this."

"Thomas, every soup kitchen, every teen night. That same lemon-sucking face. Dragging her cross and waiting for applause."

"I'm not discussing her with you."

"I've been volunteering with you three times a week for over a year. She's never even patted your hand. I'm willing to bet last night was the first time you made love in a very long time."

"We have to forget last night, and everything we said. There won't be any repeats."

"Where's the joy in your life? You see how good we are together."

Hunched into a question mark, he shut his eyes. "Please," he said, rocking, "this has to stop. We have to ask forgiveness. Let it die."

"Honey, you didn't just tell me you love me. It's my enthusiasm, my generous nature, my passion for the ministry, my beauty, my sensuality, my playfulness, my friendship. You've been thinking about this as long as I have."

"I can't do this now."

"Thomas, I love you."

Those snaring words, in her knowing, smoldering voice. They lightened his chest, dried his mouth. Same as last night, in the dark of his aging Ford. He imagined her now. Lying on her side on a sofa. Head resting on a pillow, thick brown waves fanned across it. Dancer's body in stretchy slacks. One long leg slowly stroking against the other. Both hands caressing the phone, snuggling against it, full lips brushing it. "Cynthia, there's my family—"

"Abby knows."

He hopped to his feet. "Have you done something?"

"Of course not, but she knows. Watch her next time. See how she finds reasons to get between us or pull you away."

Light spilled into the church and receded. Footsteps padded up the center aisle.

"Believe me," Cynthia said, "she knows."

"Someone just came in. I have to go."

"Thomas, come to me after Confession. I'll make us a nice dinner. Afterwards, I promise, you'll never leave."

His free hand yanked at his hair. He tented over the mouthpiece. "You're killing me!" he said in a strangled whisper.

"Everything alright?" Abby said.

He punched buttons on his phone and pocketed it before turning.

Her blandness stunned him. Pale skin, made even more ashen by the feeble lighting. Chopped, colorless hair. Androgynous slimness, a look of pure deprivation.

Clothes intended to cloak, not celebrate. She must have attracted him once.

"Who was on the phone?" she said. "You sounded angry."

Spinning away from her, he waved both arms at the ceiling. "Oh, the roofers. They want to change the price. Figured the steeple wrong, or something. But I'm holding them to the contract." He faced her again. "So, what brings you here?"

"The roofers are killing you?" Her wide eyes stared at him.

"Okay, it was a parishioner. But you know I don't like involving you in these things."

"And how, exactly, is Cynthia killing you?"

His forehead tingled. "Why would you guess her?"

"Why indeed." Head shaking, she folded her arms. "Thomas … that woman. The amount of time you spend together. The way you act toward each other. And then, of course, there's last night."

"I explained that."

"If I can see it, so can others. It's not what people expect from their pastor."

"Let's drop it. I'll tell her to stop volunteering. Okay?"

"This is very difficult," she said, dropping her gaze to the floor. "Thomas, I know I haven't given you much physical enjoyment in our marriage, but it's never meant I don't treasure you." Her eyes met his. "When we first married, I have to tell you, I was unprepared for your needs. Looking back, I suspect that one of the attractions of marrying into the cloth was believing that the spiritual life would trump the physical." She smiled and shrugged. "Silly me."

"You're a wonderful wife." Hearing himself blurt something so insipid and hollow added to the moment's awkwardness.

"My poor Thomas." She shuffled to him and kissed his cheek. "God's given you a difficult path. You're a good and gifted man, but He gave you too much passion, and me too little. I'm afraid you'll be tested throughout your life. Perhaps you'd resist better if you tried to see it that way." She grabbed both his hands and shook them. "Just remember, you're never alone."

Imagining God's witness to last night's exquisite sin doubled his shame. He wrapped her in a loose hug, held and patted her until the warmth in his face subsided.

"You can always come to me, with anything," she said, her face pressing lightly on his shoulder.

"I know. Thank you." He backed out of the embrace and kissed her forehead. "Now, let me get ready to battle those roofers."

As he watched her leave, God's disapproval turned trivial. Cynthia reclaimed his thoughts. She stepped in front of him and hooked her arms around his waist. "So," she said, smiling and rolling her hips against him, "are you man enough?"

INSIDE THE CENTER COMPARTMENT of the confessional, he clicked on the light and checked his watch. Three fifty-seven. With no penitent to deal with at the moment, he returned to a copy of next morning's sermon and whispered the text, marking the reading time on each sheet.

A wooden kneeler scraped the floor on the other side of the wall. He shut off the light and slid the little door. "When was your last confession?"

"This morning. I told a wonderful man I wanted to share his life." Cynthia pressed her wristwatch against the mesh. "It's four o'clock. You said we should talk this out when we won't be interrupted."

Lightness filled his head and chest. "Go home. We've talked enough."

"I've been thinking about us in a, I dunno, theological sort of way," she said from the shadows. "Like to hear about it?"

"There's no way we're doing this now. You've been drinking. I can smell it."

"You're right. You should drive me home. I'll ride in the back and wait for you."

"I know this is my fault," he said, "but you have to help. We're not important enough for this kind of harm. The church, my daughter, Abby."

"Bullshit."

"I can't say it any differently. I'm sorry. I should have been stronger. But this conversation is over. Everything's over."

She bolted from the booth. Seconds later his door opened and she slipped inside. Quarters were so tight he had to stand so she could close the door.

"Cyn—"

She clapped a hand on his mouth and clicked the light on. "I want to see your eyes. Eyes can't lie." Her arms slipped around his neck. "That's how I knew last night was inevitable. From the second we met, your eyes were always on me. So sweet at first. Shy, friendly, complimenting. I loved it. Then a little flirty. I liked that, too. And then they began isolating, speaking only to me, no matter who was around. Asking private, exciting questions. I did everything I could to say yes." She jostled his neck when he closed his eyes. "No, look at me. Honey, I know what you're going through. I've been divorced. It's awful. But it happens, and then everyone gets over it."

He pried her hands apart and brought them to his chest. "The clergy can't speak one way and live another. It's all for nothing if we do that. I took a vow."

"Which was okay to break last night," she muttered. "But let me ask you something. Do you think God wants us to be happy?"

"This is pointless."

"No, listen. If you promised to do something that made you unhappy, wouldn't that be displeasing to God?"

"That's just—"

Her fingers pressed onto his lips again. "And some people are made to attract certain other people. That's also part of His plan. You and me, for instance." She stroked his hands against her cheek. "Why would God make us love each other this much, only to deny us? That would be perverse. God can't be perverse."

"If I made you a promise, wouldn't you want me to keep it?"

She rolled her eyes. "Blah, blah, blah. Come up with something new."

"I've already asked God's forgiveness. Now I need yours."

"Thomas, you're the first decent—" She bumped her

fists onto his chest. "You can't show me how perfect life could be, then pull away."

"Decent man." He snorted and shook his head. "Cynthia, I'm—"

"Shhh." She cupped her fingers over his mouth and bobbed her head toward one of the confessionals.

He shrugged and shook his head.

"They're moving away," Cynthia whispered.

He reached behind her and opened the door.

A sliver of light at the church's front door went to black.

"Someone was in there," she said.

"Go home." He left her in the confessional and jogged to the front door.

"This isn't over!"

The terrace at the top of the granite steps was empty. He ambled from under the arched entryway and into the sunlight. Stretching and yawning, he pulled his eyes toward the rectory.

Abby stood on the front porch, looking his way, her hand on the doorknob. In answer to his wave, she disappeared into the house.

DIFFICULT AS IT WAS, he stayed away until the usual hour. The sound of running water in the kitchen made him raise his voice from the front hall. "Abby, I'm home."

No answer.

He heaved a few breaths before heading toward the noise. "Hi," he said when he saw her at the sink. "What smells so good?"

"Melanie made cookies for the sleepover." Back turned toward him, she twisted the faucets and grabbed a dishtowel. "It's tonight. Remember? A house full of giggly ten-year-olds. Sounds like fun, doesn't it? Will we still be a family when it's our turn?"

He stopped halfway to her. "What did you say?"

She faced him and rested her meager rump against the sink. "Do you like it?" Pale purple streaked above each eye. She had penciled eyebrows, long lashes, rusty cheeks, and lips glossed in cherry.

Arms wide, he plodded toward her. "What are you doing?"

"Answer me," she said, retreating around the small center island. "You can tell me. It's not like I'm asking what someone said in the confessional."

He stopped pursuing. "I'm sorry."

"I got to thinking after I left the church. God's difficult road for you isn't your lust. It's me. I'm your test, and it's not right. Watching you struggle. Telling you how blessed you are to face such a powerful demon." She tilted her head. "So? Am I pretty?"

"I'm so sorry."

"Stop saying that!" she said, fists and face clenched. "I'm not sure how you mean it." She let out a long breath and beamed a smile at him. Lashes flapped like they were too heavy for the lids. "Isn't now when you take me to bed?"

"Don't. Please."

"After this was finished," she said, swirling a finger in front of her face, "I was sure that's what you'd do. Soon as you saw me, you'd scoop me up and we'd make love. But then, I wasn't sure if you'd know who was in the bed. I was going to insist the lights stay on, so you wouldn't be confused. Making love with the lights on. Me. Isn't that crazy?"

"I can't do this." He turned away.

"Thomas!"

He glanced over his shoulder.

"I didn't mean to shout," she said, praying hands pressed together in front of her chest. "Am I pretty?"

"You're my wife," he said, inching toward her. "I love you, and I'm sorry."

"It's what you seem to need. Took me an over an hour. I feel clownish and pathetic, but if I'm pretty, and you don't leave …" Her hands jittered. "If this is how I stay involved in God's work …" Eyes shut tight, her mouth stretched into a wide, droopy frown. She shook with breathy, almost silent sobs.

"Abby, I'm not going anywhere." His arms circled her as if she was sunburned. "Not ever."

Arms flat against her sides, she suffered at attention.

"Let's do this." He nudged her to the sink and lifted out the whole chicken she'd been prepping. When the water warmed, he soaped a dishtowel. "Keep your eyes closed." No resistance as the cloth removed all traces of allure. His gentle strokes wiped years back onto her face. All the while, tears dribbled down her cheeks. He rinsed the towel and massaged her face. "That's better," he said, tossing the soiled cloth onto the counter.

Abby's blinking eyes roamed the room, stopping on the chicken. She lifted it by the legs and stared inside. Her breathing sped up. Tiny cries puffed out with each exhale, building to a single scream. Like wielding an axe, she raised the bird over her head and thrashed it against the counter's edge.

Frozen, he watched until the outburst ran out of steam.

Staring forward, she flipped what was left of the legs into the sink. Open hand raised in his direction, she wobbled down the hall and into their bedroom. Water tumbled into a bathtub.

Standing motionless at the mouth of the hallway, he listened until the gushing water stopped. Splashes and the occasional grunt of skin against porcelain drifted from the bathroom, overlaid with the faintest sounds of a sad woman.

He trudged through the front hall, down the porch steps, and out to the driveway. At the driver's door, he paused. A double click of the key fob unlocked everything. He slid into the back and slouched against the middle of the seat. Face tipped toward the ceiling, he shut his eyes. It was last night again. Straddling him, Cynthia's frantic hands clutched and stroked. Silky hair swept his face. Her panting rushed heat into his ears and mouth, onto his neck. Sucking, devouring kisses. Hands rode the swells of her hips. Elation from breathy declarations. His name, repeated in whispers, giggles, and gasps. Her scents and flavors. The freefall abandon.

Stomping kicks into the back of the driver's seat ended with stabbing pain in his knee. One hand massaged the leg, the other fished a cellphone from his pants. Five missed calls from Cynthia. He highlighted one. A shaky finger hovered over the *Send* button until the screen blipped to black.

Phone still in his hand, he hobbled back into the rectory. Approaching the kitchen, he recognized the thunk of slammed dresser drawers. He shouldered the back door open, clomped down two steps, and sat on the small landing. Light from their bedroom cast moving shadows on the lawn.

Elbows on his thighs, he thumbed buttons on the phone. He found *Contacts*, keyed in *c,y,n.* Her name displayed. He pushed *Options. Erase.*

Are you sure?

He shut his eyes and pressed *Yes.*

HIGHER POWER

HE'D DONE THIS every night for a week, so Grady knew where the treads creaked. Legs wide, he tacked up the former mansion's center staircase two at a time. Still on tiptoes, he made his way down the second floor hallway, to his mother's room. Only 10:30 and not even the sound of a TV passed through the few doors he passed.

The knob clicked. He eased into the dark room. Senior diapers mingled with Lysol, latex, and a Lemon Mist Stick-up in the warm air. He crept around the footboard, shook out of his quilted jacket, and draped it around the back of an overstuffed chair by the window. A groan that began in his chest escaped through his nose as he lowered onto the cushion. Sneakers came off. Crossing and re-crossing his legs, he rubbed the January sting out of each foot while he watched the slight rise and fall of the bed covers.

He pushed out of the chair and sat on the edge of her bed, one foot on the floor, the other leg bent crosswise on the blanket. Her flimsy fingers felt hot in his hand as he stroked them.

She opened and closed her eyes, chewed and sucked her lips and tongue.

"It's only me, Ma," he said in a hoarse whisper, "and you already had your dinner. Go back to sleep."

Her face ticked, twitched, and went still.

"May not be able to do this much longer," he said, his gaze wandering the room. "Think they're onto me. Especially the morning. That fat-butt, Yolanda. Each time she finds me asleep in the chair, I get a bunch of questions." He poked his chin toward the tiny bathroom. "Leaving a razor was probably my big mistake. And the clothes, I guess. Don't know if you heard her this morning, but she asked me why she found a bag of men's clothes in your closet. I sputtered something about taking them to Goodwill, but I could tell she didn't believe me. Squinted at me a good long time while she fixed your bed.

"Let's do this." He entwined her fingers and tucked the knot under the covers. After tightening the blanket around her shoulders, he leaned forward and trailed his fingers across her forehead. "I'm still sober, in case you were wondering. Six days today. How about that, huh? Ginger still won't talk to me or let me back in the house, but at the AA meetings they tell me I can't deal with that right now."

Her eyelids fluttered. A spasm yanked at one cheek.

He reclined next to her on the bed, head resting in his palm. "Hate to say it, but this AA thing is giving me a little trouble. I know the drinking is something I need help with, and they're great at that, but they're also trying to, I dunno, *force* me to be spiritual, to believe I'm part of something bigger than myself, that I have value and a purpose. They kind of hint if I don't do that, I probably won't make it.

"Everybody that gets up to talk always has some God angle. Some say 'higher power,' but it's all the same, right?

Never was much for that crap, as you know. Anyway, eventually they all get around to thanking God for a second chance at life and making things right with those they've hurt. Stuff like that."

A quick hop of his hips brought him closer. "Like," he said, his voice a little quieter, "there's this one guy who gets up a lot. Always calls himself a 'grateful' alcoholic. And that's not what you might think. He means is he's *happy* he's an alcoholic, because if he never was, he wouldn't have the sense of life's preciousness that he has today. His words, 'life's preciousness.' Kinda pretty, huh?

"Well, he said something today that really got me thinking. It was about how he knows there's a reason God let him become a drunk, and then let him get sober. All the times he probably should've died but didn't, that was all part of God's plan for him. Said now he knows his purpose for living, and what he's gonna do with the rest of his life. Never said what it was, mind you, but, Ma, he looked so happy. I hustled over to him as everyone was leaving and asked him what it was. Y'know, his purpose." He tapped the bump under her bed covers. "Know what he said?"

Her shimmery, dark eyes rolled in a slow circle. The lids closed.

"Said it was too early for me to be thinking about that. But even if I was ready, it wouldn't matter to me. It was his purpose. I'd have my own soon enough if I was willing to accept it. 'God will show you,' is all he said. Ma, he looked so happy ... But I still wish he would've told me. What'd he think I was gonna do? Steal it? Might have given me some ideas, y'know? A place to start.

"Anyway, so I spent the rest of the day thinking about

what my purpose might be. Came up with nothing. Thought about everybody I know. Everybody I've ever known. Couldn't think of what anyone's purpose was." He ran his eyes up and down her skinny outline in the bed. "Thought about you. Why you're still here, living like this. Can't be a purpose for you anymore. And even when you weren't like this, what was it? Bring one more drunk into the world?" he said, his voice rising. "That what God asked of you, Ma?"

"Sorry," he said, shaking his head quickly, "been kind of mad all day. It's that guy. He should've told me. I want to feel like he did. My whole life, I don't think I've had one day as happy as he looked today." He slapped the bed. "Why the hell wouldn't he tell me?"

She blinked and groaned.

"See, I'm not supposed to do this," he said, dropping his legs over the edge of the bed and sitting up. "My sponsor calls it 'projecting,' and it's making me anxious. He warned me. When alcoholics look too far ahead, it always goes bad. That's why I'm only supposed to think about today. Stay sober today. That's my job."

He popped off the bed and shuffled to the window. "Too much coffee at those meetings doesn't help either. Little jumpy." Fingers spread on the large pane, he rolled his forehead against the cold glass. "Speaking of jobs, I got one. Busing tables and washing dishes. Pay's terrible, but beggars can't be choosers, as they say.

"First paycheck's tomorrow. That's why I think this may be my last night here. Soon as I get that money, I'm gonna knock on Ginger's door and offer the whole thing to her. Show her I've made a new start. Let her know these last two years weren't for nothing." Eyes still trained out the window, he tipped his head toward the bed and smiled. "Be a relief to stop worrying about that fat-ass, Yolanda, kicking my foot, asking questions, giving me the stink-eye."

"Dammit," he said, shivering. He snatched his coat off the chair and put it on, shoved his hands into the pockets. "Had the shakes a lot this week." He felt a tiny wad of paper in his pocket, uncrumpled it, and squinted in the faint light. His shoulders sagged. "Oh, man. Almost forgot about this." He flapped it at her and stuck it back in his pocket.

"Credit card receipt. Ginger's Visa. Don't remember swiping it, but I do remember the liquor store clerk keeping it. Pretty sure that's why she tossed me. All kinda fuzzy, but when the guy took the card, I must have gone back to the house and raised some hell. Cops came. I do remember that. In fact, was one of the cops who got me to go to AA. Wrote a name, phone number, and address on the back of his card. Found it in my pocket the next morning when I woke up in a parked car, way the hell across town."

Arms wide, he stumbled backward and flopped into the chair. Sweat beaded on his lip and forehead. Shuddering, he hugged himself and rocked. The trembling calmed. His breathing slowed. "Man, hope that's the last of those." He pushed to his feet, crept to the bed, and kissed his mother on the cheek. "I better get some sleep. Thanks for listening, and if everything goes right, I won't see you again 'til Sunday." He mussed her wispy white hair. "Maybe I'll know what God has planned for me by then. Wouldn't that be something?"

Her tongue peeked through her lips a few times. She swallowed.

LAUGHING AND HUMMING, Grady jitterbugged with the door of his mother's room. His fingers ripped away from the knob, sending him into a heap on her floor. He crawled to the door and pushed it closed with the top of his head. Trying to make elephant trumpets with his lips came out as spitting raspberries, which made him laugh harder.

Still on all fours, he made it around the footboard and hauled himself to his feet. He crawled next to her on the bed. "It's me, Ma," he said, cheek resting on his crossed forearms. "Your no good, piece of crap son. And guess what?" He chuckled. "Yup, drunk. Knee-walkin' drunk." He lifted his head and leaned closer to her ear. "Wanna know why? Do you? Wanna know why I'm drunk tonight?" Snatching a fistful of her hair, he nodded her head and bounced it off the pillow. "Thought so."

Eyes squeezed shut, mouth gaping, she gasped.

He rolled onto his side and propped his head onto a fist. "Well, got more than one reason, really, but one big one. See, I did like I told you last night. Went to Ginger's with my paycheck and knocked on her door." His knuckles thwumped three times on the covers. "Heard her come right up to it, but she didn't open it. 'Who is it?' she said. So I said, 'Ginger, honey, it's me. Open up. Got something great to show you.' Then she said, "If you're not gone in two seconds, I'm calling the cops.'

"But I didn't leave. Walked through her bushes to the front window." He raised a wandering leg off the bed and pointed to his bloody pants. "Goddam roses. Stabbed myself like a thousand times. Guy in the liquor store asked was I attacked by a dog.

"Anyway, I slapped the check against the glass and

tapped so she'd know where to look. 'Take a peek at this, honey', I said. 'I'm a working stiff now. No drinks in a week. Pull up those blinds. You'll see a whole new Grady.'

"Well, the blinds didn't go up, but she pulled two of 'em apart." He shaded his eyes and squinted. "I could see her peeking at me. Then the slats got shoved a little wider, and a phone wiggled through. 'Cops are on their way.' Then she screams, 'And don't you ever come here again.' The blinds slapped shut, and there I was, standing like a jerk, bleeding in her goddam rosebushes.

"Couldn't believe it, y'know? Doing the right thing, and what'd it get me? Nothing." He rolled onto his stomach, folded his arms and hung his chin over crossed wrists. "Didn't want to get arrested, so I took off. Walked all over hell, even though my legs were killing me. Got pretty mad at her, just closing me off like that. Guess being mad got me thinking about everyone else I'm mad at. That AA guy, especially. Y'know, the one who found his purpose but wouldn't say. And then, by God, it hit me."

His slap on the blanket jumped her eyelids open.

"Know why he wouldn't tell me?" Teeth bared, he poked a finger at her blank stare. "He couldn't, that's why. Made it up. All of it. Just made it up. Putting on a show for all the other drunks, so we'd see what a great man he is." His arm swept in an arc. "God *himself* personally saved him, and now he's gonna be even more special than the rest of us. Bunch of bullshit.

"Sorry," he said, patting her shoulder, "but his purpose is no different than mine. Or any of those other boozehounds. Just an excuse so he wouldn't drink. Just kidding himself, like all of us."

His forehead banged a soft beat on his folded arms. "What I figure is, to be happy like that guy, I'd have to make up a lie, then force myself to believe it. And then spending all my time trying to *not* do something? How's that gonna work? I'd be a nervous wreck, then die anyway." He waggled a finger over her. "Or take over this vegetable stand. Nah, once I figured that out, couldn't get to a liquor store fast enough."

He flipped onto his back and closed his eyes. "Hey, Ma," he said, tapping her forehead, "that acorn brain of yours grabbing any of this?" His smile grew. "Acorn, that's pretty funny." He began to laugh, softly at first, then with increasing hilarity. It grew to howling, so hard he coughed in fits.

Feet on the staircase grew louder and hurried toward his end of the hall. Glare from the corridor swept into the room. A woman's silhouette paused in the light and disappeared back toward the stairs.

Shouts in the stairwell.

He struggled to sit up. Held himself upright by clasping his hands around one raised knee.

Footsteps in the hall again. Like a fat crucifix, the silhouette reappeared in the doorway.

More feet, heavier this time, rumbled up the stairs and down the corridor.

"Hey, Ma." The recoil from shoving his mother's shoulder nearly pitched Grady off the bed. "Think these jokers'll recognize two people fulfilling their purpose?"

Wide eyes trained on the ceiling, she stretched her mouth open, inhaled deeply, and squeaked.

TRAPEZE LESSON

KEVIN'S HAND SHOT from under the covers and slapped for the jangling phone. He batted the handset out of the cradle and onto the floor. Hand over hand, he reeled the receiver onto the bed, laid it on the pillow, and rolled his face against it. Each motion warned of two imminent possibilities: projectile vomiting and a cerebral hemorrhage. One eye peeked at the clock. 9:09. "Yeah," was more groan than greeting.

"Wow, Uncle Kevin, you sound like I feel." The young female voice on the other end was entirely too perky. "This is your beautiful niece, Olivia. Hope I didn't wake you."

"No ... Actually, that's a lie. Hang on a sec." He eased into a sitting position and felt for the floor with his feet. Vomiting receded from probable to possible. He raised the phone to his ear again. "Last night was fun," he said, forcing cheerfulness. "My first-ever and last-ever *mojitos*. If I remember right, you paid."

"Actually, I called to thank you. Partly for dinner, but mostly for taking the heat off me. All I've heard from my idiot sister for the past week was 'Trapeze! Trapeze!' Now that she's conned you, I'm off the hook."

Trapeze sounded familiar, but he didn't remember

being invited much less agreeing to do it. He strained to recall details of last night's many vagaries. "What are you talking about?"

"Daphne told me you said yes."

"I'm getting on a trapeze?"

"She said you agreed."

"Did you hear me say it?"

"Oh no you don't. You're not breaking that little girl's heart."

"She's twenty-eight."

"Daphne doesn't lie, Uncle Kevin."

"Olivia, even over-served, I'm not that stupid."

The other end of line remained silent.

"Point taken," he said. "Well, then I'm claiming a medical exemption."

"Baloney. You're fine."

"I don't like to talk about it."

"Uncle Kevin, you're stuck. Deal with it."

"Olivia, I'm serious. Once a man reaches fifty-five, drinking the slightest bit of alcohol after sunset causes major brain dysfunction. Mimics drunkenness. They suspect it's a vitamin D thing."

"Oh, please. You just made that up."

"You're the assistant D.A. Prove it."

"Whatever. As far as I'm concerned, you're in and I'm out. Not that I was ever in. I did volunteer to be the official photographer, but that's it. So, Uncy dearest, I'm gonna go. Meeting some friends in Central Park for a couple of loops around the Reservoir. Gotta get ready for the marathon. Want to come?"

"I'll catch up. First, some aspirin. *Adios.*" He shuffled

into the tiny bathroom of the one-bedroom sublet. Unwilling to endure incandescent light, he fumbled through the medicine chest, holding each new bottle in the faint hallway light until he located Bayer caplets. Hand-scoops of water washed down four pills. Arms propped on the sink, he inspected the haggard shadow staring out of the mirror. "Fifty-six, and still in need of adult supervision." His face moved closer to the dim reflection. Fingers traced some crags. One hand swept thinning gray hair back from his forehead and held it there. He frowned and pinched his newly-noticed wattle. Like clay, it stayed where he tugged it. "Trapeze, for godsake. No more drinks with foreign names." He slogged back to bed.

The phone assaulted him again. This time the clock read 10:16, and he felt decidedly better. "Hello?"

"Uncle Kevin, Daphne. I know Olivia spoiled the surprise, but it ... is ... on! One week from today. 9:30 AM. You. Me. The Trapeze College of NY. We'll meet at 8:30 inside the Starbuck's at Sixty-First and Broadway. I presume Aunt Stephanie will be coming?"

"I'm sorry. Who are you trying to reach?"

"Nice try. It's already on my Visa, pal. You owe me a hundred dollars and your undying gratitude."

He covered his eyes. "I don't know."

"Oh, c'mon, Uncle Kevin, admit it. You are *totally* stoked."

"Refresh my memory. Exactly when did I say I'd do this?"

"Oh, everyone had so much to drink. Who can remember all the details? Could have been as you were getting out of the cab at your apartment. I may have said something like, 'Unless you tell me not to, I'm going to reserve a spot for us in the morning.' You didn't say anything, so there you go. And we're going to have so much fun."

"Why do you want to kill a sweet old man?"

She laughed. "Hey, nobody lives forever. Go out on a high."

He squeezed his forehead. "Listen, I'm gonna go. My painkillers seem to have been distracted by this conversation. And no Starbuck's. Bunch of pinheads with laptops. Reminds me of being employed. Let's just meet at the thing. Where's this happening?"

"Trapeze College of NY. South of the Chelsea Piers somewhere. You can't miss it."

"Well, if I don't go sane in the meantime, I'll be there. And now I'm going to enjoy hanging up on you. Good. Bye."

He flipped his pillow to the cool side and nestled in for another revitalizing snooze, hoping the next time he woke he'd be able to marvel at just how vivid a bad dream can be.

"NO LUCK, HONEY." His wife, Stephanie, pointed across the street from inside the taxi. "She's here."

Daphne, wearing a white tee shirt and navy sweat pants, was doing jumping jacks on the sidewalk, her blond ponytail always a half-beat behind. The trapeze complex loomed behind her. Masts of a phantom ship, fog-bound in netting.

"Look at her, Steph. I feel like a five-year-old waiting for an injection, and she's a five-year-old on Christmas morning."

She patted his leg. "The wages of sin, darling."

"This is your fault, you know," he said as he paid the driver.

"And how's that?"

"Going to London. You know I'm no good on my own."

"Or with people." She bobbed her chin toward their niece. "We've been discovered."

Daphne spun her arm at them. "Hustle your butts," she yelled through cupped hands, "people are already in there signing up. Don't want them selling out our spots."

He and Stephanie broke into a slow trot and caught up with Daphne under the sign, Trapeze College of NY.

"Where's that sister of yours?" he said. "She told me she was going to be the photo-journalist for this historic event. If there's one thing that might come in handy today, it's a lawyer with a camera."

"I was too nervous to wait for her." She grinned and skipped a few strides. "Can't be late for school."

The second he entered the complex, his mouth dried. Viewed from inside the netting, every pole, platform and trapeze bar seemed twice as high as it did from the street. Support cables and safety lines appeared no stronger than kite string. "Steph," he said after a hard swallow, "grab a couple of those chaise lounges along the fence. I have to catch up with Daphne." He pointed to a small building with colorful *FLYER* tee-shirts tacked to the outside wall. "I saw her duck in there."

His eyes were still adjusting to the darkness when a tap on the back made him flinch.

"Thank you gigantically for disappearing," Daphne said. She pointed to a short queue. "I was on that line and whispered over my shoulder, 'Hope I don't wet my pants up there.' The person who heard that was *supposed* to be you." She steered him by the arms. "Now, stop making me embarrass myself and march to that corner. We have to sign something and put on our safety stuff."

Sporting their new accessories, they exited the shack. When Daphne saw him in the sunlight, she slapped fingers over her mouth. "I'm sorry for laughing, but you look like someone put a weightlifter's belt on the Pillsbury Dough Boy."

He pinched at flab hanging over the harness. "The girl said it should be tight." His nose wrinkled. "Pretty bad, huh?"

"Aw, who cares? Let's go find Aunt Stephanie and dump our shoes and my purse. Hopefully, Olivia's shown up with her camera." She waggled a finger at his harness. "*That* must be preserved for the ages."

"She's here," he said. "Over there with the missus." He pointed at Stephanie, who was waving her arms.

"About time, shortcake," he said to the petite Olivia. "Got your camera?"

She waved a compact digital over her head. "Let the games begin."

"Great location, ladies," he said, nodding and scanning the view. "Got the Hudson River, and a front row seat for all the death plunges." He pried off his running shoes and handed them to Stephanie. "Hang onto these, and Daphne's stuff, too. For some reason we can't wear shoes." His gaze drifted to the starting platform thirty feet over head. "Probably makes it easier to put the tag on your toe."

Clutching the things she'd just been handed, Stephanie tipped her head toward a small group forming a semi-circle in front of a tall, well-muscled instructor. "Kevin," she said, "they're doing something over there, where that good-looking young man is standing. You two have to go." As they were leaving, she kissed Daphne on the cheek. "Have fun." When he held out his arms for the same, she planted a loud smooch on his forehead and shook his shoulders. "Goodbye, darling. See you on the other side."

"Damn," he said, "was hoping to go to heaven." He trudged away, rolling an arm at Daphne. "Come along, my little assassin." She darted around him and skipped backward all the way to the man in the trapeze costume.

"Okay," the man said, clapping his hands. "All flyers who've paid and signed a release, please join me over here. My name is Royce, and we're gonna get started. We have a full class today, eight of you, so we're not going to waste time with small talk. Here's how it works, people. The first thing I'm going to do is assign each of you a number. This will be the order in which you will go through the orientation and the attempts at flying."

Kevin suspected the numbers were assigned based on relative fitness. Daphne was Number One. He was Number Eight.

"By the end of class this morning, I'm going to teach you how to hang from a swinging trapeze bar by your knees so that you can be caught by an acrobat on another swinging trapeze bar."

I can't do this. He gawked at Daphne.

Shoulders hunched, she grinned at him, fingertips clapping in front of her chin.

"Your catcher today will be me," Royce said, his eyes sweeping over the heads of the class. "The other attendants you see are here to keep you safe while you have fun. Okay. If we pace things properly this morning, you will each have three attempts to execute this exhilarating maneuver. So, relax and enjoy. Now, here's all you have to remember today. Two things. Real simple." He raised a finger over his head. "First. Legs up. Second," another finger popped up, "arms off. Told you it was simple. So, if you'll follow me to the practice bar, I'll show you what I mean."

Royce positioned himself under the trapeze, raised his arms, and appeared to levitate to the bar. "This is the 'legs up' part. Keep your ankles together. Then kick forward. Kick backward. Kick forward again. Then pull your legs through your arms and hook them onto the bar." His voice betrayed no exertion as he executed all the moves. "When you hear 'arms off', release your hands, arch your back, and reach for the catch." He re-gripped the bar, unhooked his legs, and lowered to the ground. "Make sure your hands are open for the catch. If I see fists coming at me, I'll abort. Everything looks good? You'll hear me say 'gotcha'. We're here for the 'gotcha', people. Everything else is just monkey swings. Okay then. Number One, let's do this thing."

Daphne and Numbers Two-through-Seven breezed through the land-based rehearsal.

Number Eight's jump to the bar was simple enough, but bucks, kicks and bicycling weren't enough to get his knees higher than the waist. *Better not be any pictures of this, Olivia.* Someone patted his back.

"Drop down, sir."

"Washing me out?" he said to Royce.

The instructor shook his head. "No way. Just wanted to tell you not to be concerned." He pointed to an attendant standing next to the net, holding the end of a safety line. "When Antonio yells 'legs up' during the swing, it's going to be at the point where you will literally be weightless. You'll be fine." He wrapped a huge hand around Kevin's neck and shook gently. "Relax. This is supposed to be fun. Just listen for the commands." He let go, surveyed the group, and pointed to Daphne. "Okay, Number One, it's time." Chalk clouds puffed from his taped hands as he clapped and strode toward the ladder to the platform. "You have to show this group what it looks like to fly." He smacked his hands even louder. "Let's go. Move it!"

While Daphne climbed the thirty-five foot ladder, Royce addressed the class, "Since I am still on the ground, obviously I cannot catch Number One on this attempt. This round is only so you can respond to the commands we practiced down here. So instead of being caught, today's safety line attendant, Antonio, will stop her swing with the harness ropes. He will then lower her to the net. Okay." His hands smacking together sounded like a pistol shot. "Everyone, pay close attention. Once you've climbed the ladder and attached the safety lines to your harness, the platform attendant will hook the trapeze bar and pull it toward you. They will hold your harness while you lean over the edge to grab the bar. Once you've grabbed it, you will wait for me to say 'hup.' This tells you to hop from the edge to begin your descent. Antonio will then shout the two simple instructions. Whether you're successful or not, at the end of the swing, you must remain on the bar until Antonio tells you to let go."

By this time Daphne was on her perch. Eyes wide, she blew out breaths through a mouth that had shrunken to the size of a raisin. Knees slightly bent, she held the bar and balanced at the edge of the platform.

"Okay," Royce yelled. "Fearless, intrepid Number One, here we go. Three. Two. One. Hup!"

If Kevin thought his niece was impressive on the ground, she was even better off the platform. Each maneuver was performed flawlessly and exactly on cue. Her legs moved as a unit, toes pointed throughout the flight. No hitches or lurches in any motion.

The class erupted in cheers and applause. Except for him, there was an outbreak of hopping on toes, wind-milling arms, and deep knee bends, all accompanied by smiles and encouragement to the persons in front and behind.

He strayed from the group to congratulate Daphne when she got down off the safety net.

Antonio guided her to a stop. "Would you like to do the somersault dismount?" he said to her.

"Sure."

"Okay, kick forward, backward, then forward again. Pull your knees up and let go of the bar. You'll automatically do the flip, and I'll lower you so your back hits the net. If we do it right, you should bounce back onto your feet. Go."

Daphne did the three kicks, tucked her knees and let go.

Antonio lowered her too slowly.

She landed more on her shoulders than her back, forcing her chin onto her chest. Face contorted in pain, she rolled onto her hands and knees and crawled to the edge of the net.

Antonio seemed surprised to see her immobile at the edge of the net, eyes squeezed shut. "You okay?"

"Not sure." Eyes still closed, she slowly pivoted her head side to side.

"C'mon, let's get you down." Antonio held his palms up, fingers spread. "The best way is to hook your fingers through the edge of the net and roll off head-first. You'll look like a real circus performer, like on the bar. You were really good."

She threaded her fingers under the cable, but gasped when she tried to lower her head. Some seconds passed before she inched sideways to the edge and dropped her legs over the side. Hands on her waist, Antonio eased her to the ground.

Kevin cupped a hand on Daphne's shoulder and nudged her toward the viewing chairs. "No bravado," he said as they walked. "You're going to lie down and be still for a while. And if you feel any numbness or tingling, tell me right away."

"I'll be fine."

Olivia stood and offered her chair.

Daphne waved it off. "I'm gonna keep moving. Probably better to keep it loose." She rotated her head, stopping frequently to wince or groan. Her eyes filled.

"That's it. We're done. Steph," he said, eyes on the harness buckle he couldn't remember how to unhook, "would you scare up some ice? There must be a first-aid setup around here somewhere." A hand grabbed his wrist. He looked up to see Daphne tick-tocking a finger.

"No way, mister. I'm not going anywhere until you take your turn." He opened his mouth, but she held up her hand. "Uncle Kevin, don't we always have a blast together?"

"We do. But there's no 'we' or 'together' anymore. It's

just me. Someone, you may recall, who didn't want to do this in the first place."

Her head shook even while he was making the argument. "See, that doesn't make sense. It's not like we were gonna to swing on the same bar together." A small shrug made her flinch. "Look, if we leave now, today will completely suck. But if you still do it, that'll change everything." She inched a half-step closer. "Think of it this way. Weren't you ready to do this until I got hurt?"

He nodded.

"Well, nothing's changed for you." She tapped her neck. "You're just gonna make me feel worse if you use this as your excuse."

Stephanie handed Daphne a cold-pack wrapped in Kevin's spare tee-shirt. "Hold this on it, honey."

After applying the chilly bag to her neck, she smiled and let out a sigh. "There. I'm in good hands. Don't worry about me. Just get up there and have a ball." She turned to Stephanie and Olivia. "Who else wants this fine senior citizen to risk everything for absolutely no reason?"

They cheered and applauded.

He stared at Daphne and shook his head. She'd just strapped him back onto the rolling plank to the guillotine. He blew out a noisy breath and plodded toward his classmates, unfortified by the enthusiastic, three-voiced ovation trailing after him. His knees and hands trembled during the first climb to the platform. Partial paralysis made it difficult to leave the ladder.

"Grab that bar, Number Eight," Antonio hollered from the ground, "time's a-wasting."

To his left, he was surprised to see Number Two

already at the top of the ladder and looking annoyed. He forced some deep breaths, gripped clammy hands onto the bar, and took his position at the edge.

"Hup."

The plummet stole his breath, filled his head with static. Soon as the words "legs up" entered his mind, he tried to do it. The tug on his grip was like a sumo wrestler had latched onto his ankles.

Antonio halted the swing with a pull on the safety lines. "Number Eight, did you hear me say anything?"

Twisting lazily from the bar — a piñata ready for its beating — he shook his head.

"Of course you didn't." Antonio pointed at the net. "You're pulling two G's down there." He swept the finger to the end of the desired arc. "That's why we wait until you're up there. Weightless. Next time," he said, tapping an ear, "listen." He took a deep breath. "Now, you wanna do the somersault dismount?"

"No!" He let go at the first tensing of the safety rope. On the net, he floundered onto his hands and knees, crawled to the edge, and waved off Antonio's help on the dismount. "This I can do." Fingers looped through the gaps, he gripped the thick cable, flipped over the side, and lowered to the concrete. As he headed to rejoin the queue, he located his cheering section. Each woman's face conveyed a version of *maybe this wasn't such a good idea.*

He scuffed toward the next attempt. This time Royce would be in position to make the catch. The second trip up the ladder wasn't as horrifying. Neither was the lean-away from the platform. He leapt precisely at "hup," and waited to hear "legs up," but his foot clipped the bar. Only one leg made it over. After some thrashing kicks, he got the second anchored, but the gyrations compromised the timing. Even though he heard "arms off" and stretched toward Royce for the catch, the command was followed almost immediately by a shout of "miss." This was Antonio's way of letting the catcher know that he could relax. Kevin had already heard it for several previous flyers.

Following this dismount, he saw smiles, clapping hands and pumping fists from his trio of supporters.

On the queue for his final try, he was calm enough to observe his classmates in some detail. Nobody else wore Bermuda shorts. Each wore sweat pants or gym shorts. No turkey necks, no gin blossoms, no man boobs, no spillage over the safety belt, no gray or thinning hair. Leon Russell's *Tight Rope* popped into his head. In a voice only he could hear, Kevin sang a jumble of poorly-remembered snippets as he started up the ladder.

I'm up on a tight wire. One side's ice and one is fire.
It's a circus game with you and me.
And the wire seems to be the only place for me.
A comedy of errors and I'm falling.

The word *falling* smacked of bad pre-flight juju. He wedged it from his mind and replaced it with a mantra he hoped would bring success: hup jump–legs up–arms off–gotcha.

Royce, sitting sideways on the catcher trapeze, interrupted Kevin's meditation. "You're the caboose today, Number Eight. Ready?"

He nodded, swallowed, and stared at the bar. At "hup," he launched from the platform, concentrating on nothing but "legs up." He heard a subdued cheer from the entire gallery when both legs neatly came through his arms and clamped onto the bar. At "Hands off," a kaleidoscope of concrete and netting whizzed past his upside down eyes. The swinging slowed to a frozen moment. Two arms materialized out of the ether.

"Gotcha."

You better have this one, Olivia. Locked onto Royce's wrists, he drank in the applause and whistles.

"Number Eight," a voice grunted from above.

He turned a beaming smile upward for his congratulations.

Blue, lightning-bolt veins bulged around Royce's mahogany face. "You have to let go!"

FIRST DATE

I'M STAGGERING UP the sidewalk with a passed-out girl over my shoulder. We've gotten a few doors from the house being trashed by the party. Shrieks, laughter, and ear-bleeding music are pouring through a new hole in the bay window. Last time Patty Tierney's going to tell anyone her parents will be gone for the weekend.

Sirens.

The nearest house is one I know very well. It was my grandparents' until I was about twelve. We came here every Sunday for lunch. Going to be pretty freaky hiding from the cops in their shrubs.

Ten seconds after I dump the girl behind some head-high rhododendrons, the current owners, another old couple, flip on the outside light and step out onto the concrete stoop. It's mild for October, and they stand side by side in their robes. Without a word between them, they watch fat cops with flashlights chase kids into the park across the street. We're less than twenty feet from the old man and woman. I've already prepped a smile, a wave, and a "Hi, neighbor" if one of them looks over here, or if the girl moans, or coughs, or farts – which she did while I was carrying her.

They stand there, watching until the last cop chugs into the darkness after the last kid. The old guy puts his arm around the missus. "Should've used their guns," he says and guides her back into the house. Door closes. Light goes off. It's like the old guy switched off the town.

I crab-walk backward along the cool, damp ground, until my back is flat against the foundation. The air is chilly enough to make me zip my windbreaker.

Ah crap, the girl.

I drape my jacket over her, whoever she is. First chance I've had to check her out. She's on her side, so I do the same and rest my head on my fist. Low to the ground like this, the air smells piney. Moonlight through the leaves flickers on her face each time a breeze nudges the branches. Even my Aunt Helen with the wart on her tongue would be pretty in that light. She's hugging her waist, knees drawn. Her head hangs to the ground, resting on leaves, and twigs, and earth. She's way shorter than me. Slim. Boobs are average-to-small. Short skirt's pulled tight across her hips. Epic ass.

Up on my knees, I check over my shoulders, take a quick peek at the windows. Once I'm lying beside her again, my hand glides along the outline of her body. Ribs to knee. Knee to ribs. Again. Amazing. Once again.

Her long brown hair's a mess, all full of plant stuff. Hanging upside down while I carried her couldn't have helped much either. I smooth the strands away from her cheek, pick out some of the bigger sticks and pieces of leaves.

She's totally good looking. Killer lips. An article I read said men see women's tits first. No question, but if there's a second thing, for me it's the lips. I love to kiss. Good kissing opens legs, and girls with mouths like this aren't only the best kissers, they're the ones who get excited by it. I lean close and brush mine against hers. Soft. Once more. Beer breath, but not bad. I must have it, too. One more time.

Better stop.

I sit on my heels and start revival techniques like in the movies. Soft slaps to her face don't do anything, so I shake her shoulders, rub her hands. Nothing. Pinching her lips and nose shut causes a sputter, but that's all. Snot paste on my fingers for a lousy sputter. I wipe the goo on her skirt – really fine ass – and sit next to her.

The breeze is getting cooler. Being low will keep me out of it better, so I lie next to her again. Stroke her hair. Inch my fingers to the back of her head and pull those lips closer. They're parted, so I line mine up and sweep against them.

She coughs and pokes her tongue into my chin. It's coming.

I jump out of the way and snatch my jacket off her. The first batch flies while she's still on her side, but it comes out so hard nearly all of it clears her resting spot. I scoop my hands under her waist and hoist. Heavier than she looks. She's going to have to help a little. "Put down your hands," I whisper. Nothing. Like holding a rolled carpet in the middle. "Put your goddam hands and knees down."

She does it. Gives me a chance to bounce her into a position so she's chucking toward the downslope. The barf noises are so loud, and are taking so long, I'm afraid she's going to wake the neighborhood, but no lights come on.

Still straddling her, my hands stay on her hips until she goes empty.

After I let go, she moans and starts to lie down. "Oh no you don't. You're going home." I slap her face a few times, not hard.

She tries to duck them. "Hey, you're not my father." The words are groggy and thick. She starts to cry. "You're not my father." This time tears gush out of her. In a blink, she's gone hysterical. I roll her onto her side, away from some pretty evil-smelling hurl. She goes all fetal, shuddering and holding the back of her head with both hands. Long silences hang between the breathing and the wails.

Down on my knees, I spread my jacket over her again. Feel like I should hug her or something. "C'mon. Don't cry." I stroke her hair, softly so she'll know she's okay. "You're right. I'm not your father, but I can help you find him. Tell me where you live, and I'll take you to him."

Takes a while, but the sobbing drops off to spasm-breathing. She's still not talking, though.

"I don't understand what your father has to do with any of this," I tell her, trying to sound soothing, "but I have to get you home, so I can go home. Tell me where you live."

She doesn't say anything, and I don't know what more I can do or ask. She's calmer, and I don't do anything to get in the way of that, but she keeps trying to go back to sleep. Have to poke or shake her every few seconds, tell her it's time to go home.

Takes a long time, and some squirming and groaning, but she finally sits up, legs straight out. She gets this funny look on her face when she spots me. Can't figure if she's annoyed, or scared maybe. Peeking at me every few seconds, she pulls my windbreaker tighter on her shoulders. I guess when she figures I'm not about to attack her, she rubs her face, swirls fingertips on her eyes. Her hands drop between her knees. She sticks out her tongue, tastes it, winces, and squints at me. "Where am I?"

While I'm trying to figure out what I can tell her that'll make sense, she's looking around. Her brow creases. She points to the lumpy puddle of barf. "I do that?"

"Sure as hell wasn't me."

"Stinks." Another look around. "My stuff. Where is it?"

"I don't understand."

"My purse and jacket. You got 'em?"

First time I even thought of those. "No."

"Where are they?" She seems pissed.

"Remember being at Patty Tierney's?"

"Sorta."

"They're probably still at Patty's."

"What are we doing here?" She rubs the back of her hand against her nose, bobs her chin at me. "And who the hell are you?"

"Matt O'Brien. Patty asked me to get you out of her house because the cops were coming. I carried you here, and this is where we hid." I stand and dust my pants. "You okay to walk? I gotta get you home. Must be after two, and I'm pretty tired."

"Two? Holy *shit*." She cocks her head at me. "Who are you?"

"Just told you. Matt. Your turn. Who are you?"

"Jocelyn Fontaine," she says through a yawn. "Josie."

"Why haven't I seen you before?"

"Only been here for like a month." A grimace uglies

her face. "From Oregon." She hangs her tongue over her lip. "Got any gum or mints?"

I know I don't, but tap pockets anyway. "Sorry."

She squirms her hips. "I have to pee. Got a car?"

"Yup."

Her face tightens. "Never make it." She struggles to her feet and braces against the wall. "Take off." She flaps a hand at me. "Now!"

I leave the shrubs and head toward the sidewalk.

After what seems like a long time, she stumbles out of the bushes. There's something in her hand. Two strides and down. "Shit." She manages to stand. Knees locked, she wobbles side to side. Down again. "Shit."

I jog up the slight slope of the lawn and help her up. The thing she's holding is her panties. They're covered with garden stuff and drooping like they might be wet. "Had a little problem, did you?" Can't help but laugh.

She offers them to me. "Merry Christmas."

Got to admit, I'm tempted. "Should've just left them in the bushes."

Her head bobbles as she looks around. Can't tell if she's smiling or hurting. She tugs me to the curb, opens a mailbox door, and tosses them in. "Yoo hoo," she yells to the upstairs windows of my grandparents' old house. "Panty-gram."

"Shut up." Kind of mad at her, but she is making me laugh.

We get only a couple of steps down the sidewalk and she hits the brakes. She stoops over and holds and stomach. "Feel like shit. Where's your car?"

Been afraid of that question. "Me and some friends

walked here from Sneaky Pete's. Gonna take us about twenty minutes, I'm afraid."

"Bullshit." She rips free and stumbles back toward the bushes. "Come back for me."

I race around her and press my hands against her shoulders. "You cost me enough already. I leave? I don't come back."

She slaps my hands away and staggers around me. "Just starting to like you."

"I'm serious," I call after her in a strained whisper.

Her middle finger pokes into the air. She tumbles through a gap in the bushes and hits the ground with a thud.

WITH NO CARS on the road at this hour, doubling the speed limit doesn't even seem fast. The whole trip back takes less than five minutes. Only been gone like a half hour.

I kill the lights a few houses away and coast to the curb, leave the engine running. "Josie?" I whisper near the rhododendrons. No answer, but there's snoring. I wedge sideways between two bushes and see her lying pretty much the way she was when I first pitched her back there. She's blown chunks again. Not much, but it's in her hair. I slip my hand under her neck and lift. "Wake up. Car's here. Let's go."

"What?" Her eyes bulge and wander as she raises onto an elbow. "Go where?"

"Home, soon as you tell me where that is."

I'm helping her onto her feet when the barf-caked

hair swings against her neck and sticks. Must be cold because her eyes and mouth fly open. She hangs her head at an angle and brings a handful of hair forward so she can see. "Gimme something, quick."

I look around and shrug. "Like what?"

Her head's tilted. She's wobbling on tiptoes, both hands shaking. "Hurry." Sounds like she's going to cry.

"There's nothing here."

She points at my Jim Morrison tee-shirt. "Gimme that."

"NFW, sister."

Back at the car, I toss the funked-up tee-shirt into the back seat. At least she gave me my windbreaker back. "So," I say after starting the car, "where to?"

Her head twitches as she glances around. She points forward. "Try that way."

"My fault." I squeeze my forehead. "How about this, got an address?"

"Howard Avenue. The apartments. Eighteen-eighty." She hugs her middle, nestles against the door, and closes her eyes.

"No," I shout at her. "Talk to me. Tell me about your family. Why you moved here. Stuff like that."

She tips her head back, jaw hanging.

"Stay with me." I reach over and shake her thigh. Feels amazing. "How many of you came in from Oregon? How many in your family?"

She pushes my hand off. Her eyelids stretch wide. "My mother and me. Father's still in Portland." She's rolling her head, talking all thick and slow. "She left him. Had enough and moved away. New York's really far."

"You miss him?"

"Yes," she says after a lot of nodding, "even if he was a shit. Y'know, to my mother."

But a slap in the face reminded you of him.

"So, what's your story?" she says.

"Kinda doing nothing. After my freshman year at Lafayette, the dean suggested I take a year off. Got a crummy job in Manhattan. Taking some classes. I'll probably go back next year."

No questions. No comments.

We pull onto Howard Avenue. At the apartment complex, building numbers along the street are mostly busted or missing. Only undamaged one is eighteen fifty. She flinches when I shout the number at her.

"Next one," she says, hooding her eyes. "Pretty sure."

"Hey, I know these all look the same, but 'pretty sure'?"

"God, my head." She grinds the heels of her hands into her forehead and squints through the windshield. "What's that one say?"

"Can't tell. The last two numbers are gone."

"That's it."

I park the car and open my door, but her hand slaps against my bare chest and stays there. "I'm good." She kisses her palm and waves at me, but pauses after opening the door. "Your name again?"

"Matt."

Nodding, she struggles out of the car. The passenger door bangs shut, and she rests her backside against it. Leaning forward, she pushes off from the car and staggers toward a short flight of steps, her arms spread like a little kid playing airplane. She banks to the right and topples onto a grassy upslope next to the concrete stairs.

I jump out of the car. "Stay there. Gonna kill yourself."

She looks annoyed but hangs onto my arm. We make it to her doorway. Eyes at half-mast, she pushes her open hands at me. "I got this." She wobbles close and kisses my cheek. "You're sweet." A kiss on the other cheek. "Part French. Seeya."

Not even a whiff of her barf-breath can kill the tingle from her soft kisses. "Oh no. Not after I got you this far." I hurry around her and pull the door's brass handle. Inside, there's an apartment door on either side of a small vestibule. A flight of steps leads to a landing for two more apartments. I shrug and bounce a finger at the two doors next to us.

She points up the stairs.

"Yeah, yeah," I whisper, "you're fine. Just hang onto me and be quiet."

There's some huffing and eye-rolling, but no argument. I'm kind of lugging her along as we climb to the top.

On the landing, her eyes spring wide open. She's mouthing "no key" when someone rips the door open.

A woman, her mother I guess, is in a bathrobe and bare feet. Her eyes lock onto my bare chest, then my face. She snatches Josie's arm, pulls her so close their noses touch. "Where have you been?" she says through lips that barely move. "I called the police. My God, look at you. And you *stink*."

"Mrs. Fontaine, I—"

She yanks Josie into the apartment and slams the door so hard the one downstairs puffs open. Leaves me standing there like I'm a Jehovah's Witness or something. I clomp down the steps and shoulder the door open. Halfway to the car, I stop and look back at the only lit window in the building. Behind a shade, there's two people in silhouette. One's getting a shaking and some whacks to the head. I'm shivering, but watch until the apartment goes dark. I want go back up there, kick the door in, and carry Josie out. Hold her tight and keep her forever. But I don't.

A TIME TO EVERY PURPOSE

REFILL OF PINOT NOIR in hand, Kimball checked his watch again. Vanessa was now twenty-nine minutes late. Tucked away at the corner table he'd requested, he scanned the lunchtime diners, imagining each person's reaction when she finally did show up. He caught himself in a nearby mirrored column.

Eyebrows raised, the reflection smiled, returned the nod, and offered a slight raise of the glass.

He patted the ring box bulging in a side pocket of his blazer. *To hell with them all, eh, sport?*

The image's smile faded. Its spine straightened before melting back into a slight stoop. Fingers scratched under the chin and pressed upward. Removing them drooped the skin, pelican-like.

Massaging his forehead screened away the well-dressed older gentleman. From under that shield of fingers, he spotted Vanessa at the hostess lectern. Each first glimpse of her produced the same delighted amazement.

All eyes followed her low-cut beige sweater and short navy skirt through the restaurant.

An open-mouthed smile electrified her Hollywood-pretty face. "There's my honey," she said from three tables away, both arms waving over her head, "and don't you look handsome. Blue is *so* your color." She scraped her chair next to his and leaned in for a small kiss and bite on the lip. "Sorry I'm late, angel, but I was having such a good time in the park."

Even though he'd had some himself, he smelled and tasted wine. "You let us both drink alone for half an hour, when we could have been enjoying it together?"

"I wasn't alone. This is so funny. You're gonna love it." She pawed his shoulder with one hand and pulled her hair behind an ear with the other. "So, I'm sitting outside The Boat House, letting the sun cook my face and legs." She got up and turned her chair away from the view of the other tables. "So, I was like this." Slouched in the seat, she crossed her ankles and clasped her hands on her stomach. "And you can see what happened." She nodded to her skirt, which had ridden to the top of her thighs, revealing a powder blue wedge.

He winced and fluttered his fingers for her to sit up.

"Ex-act-ly," sounded like three words. She stood, smoothed her skirt, and turned the chair back to the table. Laughing, she sat and draped an arm over his shoulder. "Well, I could sort of feel the sun on it, but I didn't realize I was flashing until I heard some guy say, 'Very nice!' I had my eyes closed, so I didn't know he was even there. Park was kinda dead, y'know? Anyway, so when I opened them, I saw him." She tilted her head back and fanned her face. "Omigod. *Gorgeous.*" Her head shook, like regaining consciousness. "So I see him, and he's giving my thong a thumb's up." Her eyes widened. A number of heads turned after she honked out a huge laugh.

His eyes darted to the blank or disapproving faces pointed their way.

"Sorry," she whispered through her fingers, "but I thought that was funny."

The waiter approached the table with another menu.

"Don't need it," she said, waving him off. "I ate something in the park. But you go ahead, angel." She patted Kimball's thigh. "I'll just have some wine and keep you company. Bring me what he's having," she said to the server. "Wait." She snatched Kimball's glass and raised a finger. "Let me just ..." A big sip brought a bigger smile. "Ooo. That's really good. Bring two. This one's mine now."

The waiter bowed and circled toward the bar.

She sipped and chewed the wine, sniffed inside the glass. "Blackberries? A little cinnamon?"

"Very good." He applauded softly.

"I have no idea," she said, smiling and flapping a hand at him. "Just repeating what you said last week. " She set the glass down and fumbled in her purse. "Better slow down on the grape juice, or this could be a short day. Where the hell did I put that? The guy was a riot, Kimball. When he saw the goods, I guess he thought I was presenting or something. Anyway, he just walked right up to my table and sat down. We got to talking, and he bought me a couple glasses of chardonnay. Horse wizz compared to this stuff. What is it?"

"Pinot noir." He pressed back into the chair. "You ate? We're here for lunch."

"It was a while ago." She continued to rummage in her purse. "I'll have a salad or something. Ah, here it is."

He ignored the business card she held in front of his nose.

"Captain Andy Ventarella," she read aloud, "Charter Operator. Said he runs a fishing boat out of Point Pleasant." She held the card out again. "C'mon, angel, you're not playing right. This is where you get jealous." Her ring finger wiggled at him. "Bet a special something here would scare away those nasty men."

He twisted in his chair, blocking the ring bump from her line of sight. "My daughters tell me I've lost my mind. I embarrass them."

"This again?" she said, rolling her eyes. "Screw 'em. They're just afraid you'll have fun, live a long time, and blow their inheritance."

"I get the feeling my friends are avoiding me."

"Angel," she said, stroking his hand, "you care too much about bullshit. The men are envious, and their old bag wives are afraid the husbands will want what you've got."

"Or," his head rocked side to side, "maybe there really is 'a time to every purpose unto heaven.'"

Eyes narrowed, she shrugged and shook her head.

"The Bible. Ecclesiastes. My time for you is past."

"Screw the Bible. Are you happy? I know I am."

He smiled, tugged the captain's card from her fingers, and spun it onto a bread plate. "Commanding one of the larger rowboats on the lake was he?"

"There, that's better." Grinning, she licked the rim of her wine glass. "God, you're sexy. Think anyone would notice if I ducked under the table?"

"Let's stay on point for a second, shall we?" He tipped away from her. "I have to tell you, I don't like cooling my heels for half an hour while you have bad chardonnay with a stranger. And no call?"

"Oh, don't be mad. The guy bought me some wine, and we talked about the beautiful day. I lost track of the time is all. What do you think I was doing? Giving him a little sumthin sumthin in the restroom, for godsake?" She pulled him toward her. "Don't be like this. You know I love you." The backs of her fingers trailed across his cheek and hair.

He stared, remained silent.

She massaged his neck. "C'mon, we have the whole day and night ahead of us. Don't spoil— Ooo, Kimball, look."

His eyes followed hers to a woman with shopping bags piled around her ankles.

Blinking accompanied Vanessa's pout. "She's been to Henri Bendel. I wanna go, too. After lunch, can't we do just a *little* shopping?"

"Nest for hours in one of those pathetic 'husband' chairs? I hardly think so."

"Aw, please? We have all afternoon." She bounced her eyebrows. "We can go to Victoria's Secret. I'll model a few things for you later."

Nose crinkled, he shook his head. "Sounds a bit smarmy, even to me." His eyes swept the room. "One more venue to be seen as a salivating letch."

Her fist banged into his arm. "Stop doing that. You're not too old, and there's nothing wrong with us being a couple." She straightened in her seat, rocked her hips, and glared around the restaurant. "And if anyone doesn't like it," she said, her voice rising, "they can go screw themselves." She shook his forearm and tipped her face in front of his. "That's what you should be thinking too. We love each other, so screw 'em all." She twitched her nose at him and smooched the air.

"You're really quite extraordinary, child," he said, smiling.

"God, I love it when you call me that." She beamed and hugged her middle. "How? How am I extraordinary?"

"Well, for one thing, you've made me reconsider whether Providence truly exists." His fingers brushed across her cheek. "When Mimi died, I saw myself leading a very different life, one that would become progressively smaller and more insular. Now I see possibilities. I'm happier than I've been in ages."

"Me, too." She clinked her glass against his and took a healthy sip.

"*Salut.*" Setting the wine down without drinking, he dropped his gaze into the glass. "Of course, you're right about it being my life, my choices. But that doesn't mean I'm unaware of the absurdity of … us. Two souls traveling in non-parallel universes. No plausible tangents or bisects. Yet, here we are." He tapped a finger to the side of his nose and lowered an eyelid. "And I believe I know why."

"I can actually feel my brain getting bigger when I listen to you," she said, inching closer.

"The joy of living comes from surprises. We're so opposite, everything's a surprise. At least to me. I have no idea what you're going to say or do. Ever. And then whatever it is, I find it delightfully exotic. Even the vulgarity is somehow endearing. It's earthy. Untamed."

"Oh really?" Her eyelids flapped. "You find me vulgar, you douche bag?"

He laughed. "I do. But it's oddly good natured. There's a spontaneity, a playfulness. It's energizing just to be around you." He leaned so close their foreheads touched. "And the love making. Astonishing."

"I know." She purred. "It's why I like mature men. So patient and attentive. And, omigod, great hands." Her eyes and mouth opened wide. "My ex? One time I caught him watching a baseball game over my shoulder."

"Mimi wouldn't have dreamed of doing the things you do. I doubt she even knew some of them existed." He chuckled. "Not sure I did."

"Time to forget Mimi," she said, fingers scratching lightly on his back. "You have me now. And don't worry that I'll dry up and sprout a mustache. There are lots of ways to fool the clock these days. I'm gonna stay as young and pretty as your money and medical science can make me. I see us having a terrific twenty years, maybe—"

"Sssh." He pressed a finger to her lips. "No math. Remember?"

"Sorry." She wrapped her fingers around his hand, kissed the tip of his shushing finger, and sucked it into her mouth up to the big knuckle.

He yanked the hand onto his lap and scanned the room. Unable to suppress a laugh, he turned to his giggling companion. "There's a time and a place, you lunatic."

"You are such an adorable tight-ass. I just love you." Her knee jostled the table when she bounced toward him, arms wide. Wine slopped from her wobbling glass as she grabbed it. A ripple splashed onto the table, strafing droplets across her beige top. "Son of a *bitch!*"

The room quieted. Patrons twisted and glared. Kimball's small wave and shake of the head halted the waiter's advance. Elbow on the table, he rubbed his forehead and gazed around the room, stopping on Vanessa, who was dabbing a moistened napkin on the maroon flecks.

"I'm going to have to take this off." She downed the rest of her wine and slid the empty toward him. "Order me another, angel. I'll be right back." A bit unsteady, she headed toward the Ladies.

He dabbed his napkin at red speckles on the dinnerware. After patting the bread dish, he noticed he'd smeared something handwritten on the captain's business card. Reading glasses on, he saw a phone number with "cell" next to it. On the back, someone had written "Ay Caramba!" and underlined it twice. Tapping the card on the table, he rubbed his lips and peeked toward the Ladies. He loaded the "cell" number into his phone and returned the card to the plate. Heading for the lobby, he spun a finger at the waiter for another round, pushed *Send,* and pressed the phone to his ear.

"Yo," a deep, New York-y voice said after the third ring.

"Captain Ventarella?" he said.

"Who's this?"

"I work with Vanessa, the woman you met in Central Park this morning."

"Wow."

"Wow, indeed. Anyway, as luck would have it, she knows I've been considering putting together an employee fishing outing, and she just gave me your card. She was emphatic that I give it back to her, but somehow I smudged the handwritten number. I was mostly calling to test if I was reading it right."

"We're talking aren't we? But don't hang up. So, you're interested in a charter? That's great. How big and when?"

"Not sure yet. By the way, I noticed someone wrote 'Ay Caramba!' on the back of the card. Is that the name of your boat?"

"Name of the boat," the captain said, laughing, "that's great. Nah, it's from *The Simpsons*. You know, on TV? It's what Bart says all the time when he's blown away by something. Turns out she and me both like the show, and … How well do you know that wild woman?"

"Very. She was sort of a side dish for a while, until the wife got suspicious. We've stayed close though, and I can understand any man saying 'Ay Caramba!' after meeting her."

Another laugh burst through the phone. "Yeah, well, there's a little more to it than 'Ain't she pretty.' But you know what I'm talking about."

"Maybe yes, maybe no." He swallowed away some dryness. "Sounds like something happened after the wines."

"I never met anyone like her. Crazy, y'know? The kind that gets off on the danger, I guess. She ever do that with you?"

"Not sure. You'd have to tell me what happened." He tilted the mouthpiece away from the sound of his open-mouth breaths.

"Well, we finished a second glass of wine, and she tells me she's gotta be somewhere, but then she gives me this funny look and says, 'Bet I can get an 'Ay Caramba!' outta you.' I ask how, and she takes my hand … Forget it. Must still be a little buzzed. But hey, call me soon as you know about the boat. Okay?"

"Captain, she and I had almost two years together. Nothing she does could shock me."

"Nah. The two of you. Same office and all. I can't."

"I, uh, may be in the market for two charters. Create a little competition between departments. C'mon," he said, fist thumping against his thigh, "don't leave me hanging."

"Just between us?"

"This must be really good."

"Gotta promise you won't say nothin'."

"Absolutely."

"Where was I?"

He covered his eyes. "She took your hand."

"Right. So she's got hold of my hand, then she says, 'Come with me. I want to thank you for the drinks.' Next thing I know, we're in a stall in the ladies' room, and I'm brushing her teeth but good. She got her 'Ay Caramba!' and then some. But you been there. You know what I'm talking about … Buddy, you still there?"

"Sorry. Look, I have to go. I'll—" He killed the call and bent toward the floor. Waiting for his face to uncoil, he ran a licked finger across the tips of his shoes, picked phantom lint off his cuffs. A host of "told you so" faces swarmed in his skull. He took a step toward the revolving door, but pivoted and returned to the dining room.

Vanessa and the new wines were waiting at the table. She patted his chair. "Put it in there, big boy. I missed you." Arms wide, she pushed her breasts out. "Pretty good, huh? Had to take it off and use the blow dryer on the wall. Got a few looks, but screw 'em." She picked up her wine and smiled. "So, where'd you go? Men's room?"

He eased into the chair. "Couldn't find a date."

Her eyes flicked sideways at him as she carefully set the wine on the table. "That's certainly an odd thing to say." She laughed. "Is this your way of telling me you're gay?"

"I was thinking about you while you were gone," he said. "How magnetic you are. How people are drawn to you. It's quite remarkable, really."

She batted her lids and smiled toward the ceiling. "What can I say?"

"Your charter captain, for instance. Seems a decent fellow."

"Nice enough, I guess."

"Oh, be generous, Vanessa. He raved about you."

Her eyes darted from him, to the card, to him. "What are you talking about?"

"Ay Caramba's."

"You're not making—"

"Give it up. Your foolish joke about being late matched his version exactly."

"You called? You're checking up on me?"

He shrugged.

Facing away, she bobbed her head in time with the beat of her tapping heel. "So you know," she said, turning back to him. "So what? No big deal anymore. Like a ... a goodnight kiss in your day. And you don't own me. You want me all to yourself?" She stroked her ring finger.

A laugh puffed through his nose.

Bravado drained from her face. "Aw, don't be mad, angel. It didn't mean anything. Too much to drink on an empty stomach. That's all. Forgive me?"

He recoiled from her reaching hands. "You must be quite a favorite. Regaling your friends with stories of how you play me. Clueless old jackass, waiting patiently for his turn while you entertain the park." He banged a finger on the captain's card. "But this was reckless. Taunting me, like a murderer sending riddles to the police. Not a particularly bright thing to do to a lawyer, child."

She snatched his hand with both of hers. "You're making way too much out of this. I love you. Just you."

He swiped her hands away and pinched a pair of one hundred dollar bills from his billfold. Laying them on the table, he winced and laughed. " 'Ate something in the park.' I just got that. You really were having fun with this." He patted the money and pushed away from the table. "That should more than cover everything."

"One more chance? Kimball, please. I'm sorry."

"I wish you a happy life." He bowed and left her staring at the cash, her lips pressed tight, nostrils pulsing, sadness pooling in confused eyes.

Out in the glowing October afternoon, he ambled up Fifth Avenue and into Central Park. Occasionally, he fingered the felt-covered box, or secreted a handkerchief to his nose and eyes. Her heartbreak seemed genuine, making his that much more bewildering.

Unhurried wandering found him at the Boat House, scene of her good manners and mortal sin. He imagined leaning against the outside wall of the Ladies, holding her purse, waiting for gratitude to run its course. A modern man, in sync with trends, not a time traveler abandoned in the future.

THE THINGS WE DO FOR LOVE

OLDER BROTHER, BRENDAN, bumped a shoulder into him. "For crissake, Eddie," he whispered, "a little respect, huh?"

"Stinks in here," Eddie said, continuing to read the underside of his necktie. "What is it with dead people and lilies?"

"Hey." Brendan tapped him on the arm this time.

"Leave me alone," he said, banging back with an elbow.

"Look up, stupid. Your ex just came in, with Brittany."

His eyes shot to the arched opening of the viewing room. He straightened and smoothed his tie, pulled his shoulders back, and slapped on a smile.

"Kid of yours is growing up pretty as her mother," Brendan said.

Eddie's ex, Melissa, led their daughter toward the casket where he was standing. Brittany skulked so closely behind her mother, she bounced backward when Melissa stopped a few feet from him.

He smiled at the half face peeking around his ex-wife. An unblinking eye, like the other side of a keyhole, stared back at him.

Melissa hugged her shoulder bag with both arms and raised her chin. "I'm sorry about your father, Eddie. I liked him very much."

"Thanks for coming. You look fantastic." He reached for her, lips puckered.

She lurched backward, knocking Brittany off balance. "Have you lost your mind?" Head shaking, she tented a hand over her eyes. "Un-be-*lievable.*"

"What?" he said, arms still outstretched.

Eyes wide, she exhaled through an open-mouth. "So, had he been sick long?"

"Not a day." His fingers fanned across his throat. "Choked on a piece of steak, actually."

"Oh, how horrible. So sad when someone dies alone like that."

"Wasn't alone. He was at my apartment."

Confusion grew on her face. "Were you there?"

"Yeah, having dinner."

"Then how could—"

"It's not what you think," he said, wagging a finger. "Wasn't like he just dropped face first onto the plate. We were eating. He got up and left the table without saying anything. That's it."

Head shaking, she shifted to her other foot. "You couldn't see what was happening?"

"I didn't know. Thought he didn't like the food, or maybe the company. Never occurred to me to go looking for him. I finished mine and went to the bathroom. There he was, lying on the floor. Very blue. Very dead."

"Such a tender rendition. Still a charmer, I see." She squinted at him. "You didn't hear anything?"

"I'm supposed to think every little thump is an old man choking to death?"

"God, that poor man."

"Yeah," he said, extending his arms again.

She reached behind and yanked Brittany between them, both hands on the young girl's shoulders. "Don't you have something to say to your father and Uncle Brendan, honey?"

"Sorry about Grampa FitzGerald." Her eyes circled from him, to Brendan, to her feet, then back to him.

"Gimme a big squeeze, Britty." Eddie stretched his arms for her.

"It's Brittany," she said, bending forward, arms at her side. Her cheek tapped his chest once before she pushed out of the hug.

"Aw, not my Pretty Britty anymore?"

"Yuk." When he stroked her hair, she stiffened and glanced at her mother.

"You didn't get to see him very often," Eddie said, "but your grandfather loved you, y'know."

Lips pressed together, Brittany shrugged, bobbled her head, and caught her mother's eyes again.

Melissa raised her chin toward the casket. "Let's go say a prayer for Grandpa Fitz—"

"Whoa." Eddie propped both hands against Brittany's shoulders. "Gimme a second, will you?" He ran his eyes over his daughter. "Haven't seen her since she became a woman."

Brittany froze, eyes pointed at the floor. "Mother?"

"Stop it, Eddie." Melissa said.

"Britty, it's okay. I'm your father."

The young girl slapped his hands away. "My name is Brittany!" Glaring at her mother, she backed toward the casket.

"You're amazing," Melissa said to him.

"Wow," he said, gaze fixed on his daughter, "she grew up overnight. You could be a grandmother, Melissa. Wouldn't that be a pisser? Grandmother at thirty-one."

"Should've killed you." Her clenched teeth never parted. "In fact, I'd like to do it right now."

Brendan edged his big body closer to them. "Easy now."

"She didn't call me Daddy," Eddie said, without taking his eyes off Brittany. "How come? You been saying things about me?"

"Are you on crack?" Melissa said, laughing without a smile. "You spend three days with her in five years, and she's expected to think of you as Daddy? You're lucky she remembers you exist. The only way I got her here tonight was to promise we'd go to the mall afterward."

"Does she call your new husband Daddy?"

"You're insane," she said, her voice rising.

"That's enough." Brendan wedged between them. "Wrong time. Wrong place."

Eddie raised his open hands. "Okay. You're right." His face broke into a smile. "Hey, the newspaper had a nice picture of you and that older fellow you married."

"*That*," she said, eyebrows raised, "was more than three years ago."

"Well, this is the first chance I've had to talk to you. What's his name again? Carter?"

Nodding slowly, she studied his face.

"So, tell me how you like getting banged by your father."

"Knock it off." Brendan pressed an elbow into Eddie's chest.

Melissa's lips thinned, nostrils widened. "Carter's nine years younger than my father, Eddie," she said, voice trembling, hands curled into white-knuckled fists, "and a hundred lifetimes from you." She grimaced and shook her head. "I'm not letting you do this. I came here to teach Brittany something and to show respect for your father. He was the only one in your family who was ever kind to me." Sliding sideways, she grabbed Brendan's hand and crinkled her nose. "I'm sorry. I didn't mean you."

"I know," Brendan said. "Thanks for coming. Couldn't have been easy. Nice to see you and Brittany again. You really do look amazing."

"Thank you. Finally being happy probably has a lot to do with it." She patted the back of Brendan's hand and headed toward the casket.

"Look at that butt," Eddie whispered. "No, don't. You shouldn't be having thoughts like that about my wife."

"Ex-wife."

"There's still something," he said, grinning.

Brendan slapped him on the forehead. "Does the real world ever intrude in there?"

"G'NIGHT, VALERIE," Brendan called to his wife as he and Eddie clomped down the narrow stairs to Brendan's basement. "Decent crowd tonight," he said. "Don't you think?"

"Guess he fooled some people," Eddie said. "Wonder how many'll show up tomorrow for the planting?" He paused near the bottom of the steps and covered his nose. "God damn, Brendan. Place needs a dehumidifier. Or some other kind of fire."

Brendan squatted in front of a dorm-sized refrigerator and took out two beers. "Couple of these and you'll convince yourself it's beaver. That's what I do."

"Really?" he said, laughing. "Been a while. Can I live down here?"

"No."

"Wow, that was quick."

Smiling, Brendan handed him a beer. "In case you weren't kidding."

"Hey, jumbo, remember that Thanksgiving I came home from Amherst?" He dropped into a broken recliner and loosened his tie. "You picked me up at the bus station and crashed into a pole?"

Brendan flopped onto the couch. A sparse cloud of dust rose and glittered in the fluorescent light. "What the hell brought that up?"

"The old man, and seeing Melissa." He squeezed the back of his neck. "That was a weird day for me."

"What isn't?" Brendan clunked his feet onto a plastic coffee table.

"See, I was planning something special that day, so I remember almost every detail." He sat forward and dropped his gaze to the floor. "We're driving down Decatur Street. You drop a lit cigarette between your legs, lift that fat ass off the seat, and grope for it."

"I wasn't fat then."

"Your foot slips onto the gas, and boom. Ambulance. They keep you. I go home."

"Where's this going?"

Eddie knitted his fingers together. "Like I said, it's about the old man and Melissa, and what I'd planned. Something I never told you before."

Sitting forward, Brendan rolled his hand at him.

"Okay, that night you stayed in the hospital, we finished dinner and the old lady went down to the basement. I needed a ride to Melissa's, so I went down there to ask. She was doing laundry, which reminded me my suitcase was still in the trunk of your wreck. When I told her, she insisted I get the old man, go right down to the body shop and check through the whole car." He bumped the heel of his hand to his forehead. "Brendan, this next part's so clear it could've happened today. I go into the TV room. He's lying on the couch, asleep. I swear, he looks dead. I mean, exactly how he looks in the box right now, but his mouth isn't sewn shut. It's hanging open. So I get pretty close. He's breathing, but real shallow. Lots of gurgles and wheezes. I'm sorta hypnotized, waiting for the bastard to die, right in front—"

"Let it go."

Eddie flipped up his middle finger. "The only reason I wake him is so he can drop me at Melissa's after the body shop. Y'know, for this thing I was going to do."

"That's twice. What's the big mystery? What plan?"

"In a minute. So I shake him, kinda rough. He jack-knifes. Swallows a snort. His teeth clack together hard. Sounds like a break shot in eight ball. His eyes are bloodshot. They're all wild and wandering. Of course, he's steaming. And when I tell him the old lady wants him to go get *my* stuff from *your* trunk, he rubs his face and says, 'You guys are two loads that should've gone in the sink.' "

Brendan slapped a hand over his eyes and laughed, then thumped a fist onto his chest like he'd taken an arrow. "Ow. You I can see. But me?" He squinted. "You just made that up."

"C'mon, you must've heard him say that."

Brendan shook his head.

"What about, 'You're as useless as the Pope's nuts?'"

Another head shake.

"'You're gonna make somebody a fine wife some day?'"

Another head shake, plus a shrug. "Guess he saved his best stuff for you."

He squeezed a hand over his eyes. "Yeah. I was the favorite, alright."

"Shut up." Brendan slid his hips to the edge of the cushion. "We're not going through that again. Y'hear me?"

"How would you—"

"I said shut up!" Pitching even closer, Brendan stabbed a finger at him. "He's dead. Change the subject." Slowly, he fell back against the cushion. "How 'bout you get back to that plan thing you were telling me?"

Eyes to the floor, he shook his head. "You don't care."

"C'mon. You got me curious. So, you and the old man have to go out and ... then what?"

"Okay," he said, sitting taller, "so we drive to the body shop. After we get my suitcase from the trunk, he's going through the car and finds Valerie's panties in your glove compartment."

"Whoa. Whoa." Brendan popped forward, eyes to the ceiling. "She doesn't know that happened."

"Like it matters now. Anyway, I can tell the old man's super embarrassed. He gets out of the car but won't look at me. Just launches into this story about how he was young once, feeling the same urges you and I feel, but getting a girl pregnant would ruin a man's life. And then he tells me about this date he had one night. They were parked in his car. She wanted to do it, but he said no. So she took his keys and dropped them inside her blouse. Told him if he wanted them, he'd have to go in after them. Then, with a straight face, he tells me he got out of his own car and walked home."

"Oh, yeah," Brendan said, laughing, "that's exactly how it would happen."

"Felt like spitting in his bullshit face, but that wouldn't get me to Melissa's. So I thanked him for the talk. The bastard shakes my shoulder and says, 'Eddie, you're a pretty good kid, sometimes.'"

Brendan hopped off the sofa and headed toward the fridge. "See, he wasn't all bad."

"Oh, yeah, a saint. Must've shocked the shit out of him to wake up in hell yesterday."

Back at the sofa, Brendan belched and rubbed his stomach. "I'm going to bed after this one, and you're going home. Get to the goddam plan already."

Eddie dinked a fingernail against the bottle and flicked his eyes at him. "Brendan, I knocked up Melissa that night. On purpose. All that crap the old man was saying? The whole time, I knew I was gonna do it."

"Jesus Christ."

"Had her cycle all figured out. Cut the tip off a rubber

and stuck it back in the foil. Ten minutes after her mother went to bed, we made Brittany in her kitchen." His gaze bounced between Brendan and the floor. "Say something."

Brendan sat on the edge of the sofa, eyes drifting. "For godsake, why?"

"I was losing her. Could pick it up when we'd talk on the phone and in her letters. Lots of stuff about how great college was. All the things she was learning. The new people she'd met. Places they were from. How she planned to visit them during breaks. Stuff like that."

"What did you think was going to happen? And how's that different from when you went away to school?"

"Had to get her away from that place. Always knew we'd get married. Figured it would be farther down the line, but that began to look too chancy. She'd never consider an abortion, so if she got pregnant, she'd leave school, marry me, and we'd start our life."

"You've always been messed up, Eddie, but this … Jesus."

"Can I have another beer?"

"Help yourself. Tell me something," he said as Eddie headed for the fridge, "how does this square up with you trying to lift every skirt in town right after the wedding?"

"Yeah, that. Kinda made a little … miscalculation." He shuffled back to his chair and fell in. "About a week after we got married, I was helping her with the dinner dishes. We were talking and laughing. Having a real good time. Everything felt just the way I thought it would. Perfect. Then, I don't know why, but I thought she'd love me even more if she knew how I'd planned everything. Thought it would show her how important she was to me."

"Wow. Not bright."

"No shit. She stared into the sink for a few seconds, then scooped out a knife and came at me. I grabbed her wrists, but she wouldn't quit. The only thing that made her stop was me yelling, 'The baby! You're gonna hurt the baby!' She backed away, but threw the knife at me." He undid a cuff button and bunched the sleeve above his elbow. "Hit me right here," he said, pointing to his forearm. "Gashed more than stuck."

Brendan inspected the L-shaped scar. "Holy crap."

"Hurt like hell. So, I chased her, but she raced into the bedroom and locked the door. From that minute on, everything was different. She wouldn't talk. Cried a lot. I'd come home from work, and she'd be sitting on the couch, hugging a pillow to her middle. Wouldn't even look at me. And sex? Stopped," he snapped his fingers, "just like that. Hell, I was only nineteen. Could've done it five times a day. What'd she think was gonna happen?" He pumped the air with his fist. "I don't think so."

"I've had a couple beers, Eddie, but I think this is a real question." He leaned closer. "Are you crazy?"

"What do you mean?"

Brendan placed his empty on the table, slapped his thighs, and stood. "Forget it. I'm going to bed."

"No." He jumped to his feet and blocked the path to the steps. "Tell me why you said that."

"Okay. You wreck her life and expect her to be grateful? I'd call that's nuts. How could you think you were doing her a favor?"

"Because it was. No one could love her like I do. Ever."

"That's—" Brendan cocked his head. "Did you say 'do'?"

He sat, arms lying across his knees. Eyes shut, he drew circles on his temples. "She hasn't been out of my head in thirteen years. Not one minute." Both hands slid to the top of his head and rubbed to the rhythm of his rocking. "When I'm not at work, a lot of times I get in my car and find her. Got this notebook of what she does, so it's pretty easy. She can be anywhere. Gym, dry cleaner, hair, nails, school, doctors. Got it all."

Brendan lowered onto the sofa. "I'm almost afraid to ask. What do you do when you find her?"

"Watch her," he said, smiling. "Just watch. Got this little pair of binoculars in the car. Only get close enough that I can see her face clearly. Try to share her moods. She smiles. I'm happy. She frowns. I'm mad. When she's on her cell? I hold mine to my ear and pretend she's talking to me. Feels like we're a couple again."

"And you don't see that's sick?"

"Not hurting anyone."

"Not doing any good, either."

His face tightened. "Here's the good. That old man she married. That Carter. He's gonna die soon. I figure the more I know about her, the easier it'll be to get back in her life." He shrugged. "In the meantime, I get to see her. That part, right there, is good enough for me. For now."

"I'm at a loss here," Brendan said, shrugging and shaking his head.

"I know what I'm doing."

Brendan dropped to one knee, cupped a hand on the back of Eddie neck, and shook gently. "Eddie, listen to me," he said. "She wouldn't piss on you if you were on fire. At least now I know why. You're not getting her back, and this is too weird, even for you. You need to see someone."

"Who knows her better?" he said, knocking the arm away and sitting up. "You or me? She loved me once. I can make her do it again. When Carter dies, I'll need to take things a little slow. I know that. But I *am* going to get her back."

Brendan's face drifted in front of his until their eyes locked. "And why, exactly, is Carter going to die soon?"

"People die, Brendan," he said, a smile creeping onto his face. "Just have to be patient. Got to see the old man croak, didn't I?"

GRAVITY

A LONE, DETERMINED BUG dinked against the single overhead bulb. Under that cone of light, each man anchored an end of a small bench at the station. They sat hunched forward, arms lying across spread knees, eyes trained on the ancient grime and blackened gum wads that speckled the concrete platform.

"Gonna talk to me or not, Mikey?" Ralph said to him. "Thought that's why you asked me to wait with you."

"Trying to get the words right," he said, eyes still down.

"Just talk. They'll come. You been too quiet through this whole thing. Not good."

Mike's head dropped lower. Both hands rubbed his hair. "Think people can make themselves die?"

"Jeez, let's not— You mean Jeremy?"

"Anybody."

"Where you going with this?"

"There was this TV show about prisoners of war. Pretty sure it was Korea. They said guys went to sleep and died. No reason. Couldn't take it anymore and *made* themselves die." He glanced at Ralph, then back between his feet. "Sound possible?"

"He's buried, Mikey. It's over. Time to talk about

other things. Better yet, let's go back to the house." Ralph backhanded him across the shoulder. "Which is where you shoulda stayed for this whole thing. Commuting was stupid. Far as Rosalie and me are concerned, you're still family." Palms pressed to the edge of the bench, Ralph leaned forward. "C'mon. I'll call and ask her to make up a bed."

He shook his head and stayed seated. "No. You're great people, but no. Go ahead home. This was a mistake. You won't understand."

"Understand what?" Ralph said, annoyance creeping into his tone. "You're not saying anything. C'mon, let's go."

"No." He stood, wandered to the yellow border of the platform, and studied the silent darkness in both directions.

"Something coming?" Ralph said as he caught up.

"Got about ten minutes, maybe more. It's been late every night."

"You still going then?"

He nodded.

"Stubborn." Ralph pulled a wad of bills from his pants pocket. "How about money? Y'okay?"

"Thanks, I don't need money."

Ralph snapped a fifty out of the stack and pushed it at him. "G'won, take it. Get yourself a bloody steak. You look terrible."

"No. I'm good." Turning his back to the cash, he shuffled to the bench and plopped onto the seat.

Hands stuffed in his pockets, Ralph stayed by the tracks, staring at the rails. "Know what I remember most, Mikey?" He glanced over his shoulder, half of his mouth pulled into a smile. "Candyland. Believe that? Candyland."

His gaze returned to the tracks. "Played it with him for hours on the bed. Even being so sick, all skinny and pale and everything, little guy could still laugh. Rips your heart out."

"He did love that."

"I know I been a broken record about this, Mikey, but how could he be all happy and cheating at Candyland, then gone a week later? Those doctors, they messed up." He sawed a finger under his nose. "Not right. Somebody gotta check into that."

"They got him two extra years."

"No. He was getting better," Ralph said over his shoulder.

"Let it go. Gravity won. Gravity always wins."

"What the hell's that supposed to mean? Jesus, Mikey, sometimes ..."

"We're born, we struggle against gravity, and then we lose. Jeremy lost."

"Gravity shouldn't beat a four-year-old. That's bullshit. Those doctors." Ralph tipped his face away, shook a finger at him.

"And what if they did mess up? What then? We sue for millions? Now *there's* some fine cash. Let's see, Porsche for me. Molly and her boyfriend go to the Caribbean every June the seventh. Hold hands on the beach. Toast Jeremy at sunset."

"You don't have to get like that. And what boyfriend? All my daughter's done for two years is work and take care of that little boy."

"There will be," he said, barely above a whisper. "At least I hope there will."

Ralph returned to the bench. "Don't you want her back?"

"What? That's not gonna—" He flinched. "What?"

"Near the end, when Jeremy was so sick, you and Molly, together, with him. Maybe I'm crazy, but I thought I saw something."

"Not 'maybe', Ralph."

"Rosalie saw it first. I guess mothers have an eye for that stuff. She got me looking for it, and I'm telling you, every now and then, Molly's eyes, they'd follow you. She'd get this little smile. Know what I'm saying?"

"I put Molly through three years of hell. Why would you want her to risk more of that?"

Ralph's eyes glistened, nostrils pulsed. "Nothing happens by accident. Something good has to come from this."

"Jeremy's not in pain anymore, and Molly's finally free." He held his fingers in a vee. "That's two good things." Another finger popped up. "And everything comes in three's."

"No, something better than that." Ralph sat, hips angled toward him. "See, Rosalie and me, we thought with you off the junk, and Jeremy being gone now, well, maybe God's plan was, you know, for the little guy to bring you and Molly back together. A new life from the ashes, kinda."

"So, God tortures and kills children so people will kiss and make up?"

"Mikey, don't." Ralph's thick hand curled into a fist. "That terrific little boy." Clenched teeth showed through thin lips. "I need a *reason*."

"When Molly and I split up, she never told you much, did she?"

Pressing his back against the bench, Ralph wiped a wrist across each eye. "Never was the kind to run to mommy and daddy. We could see you had, you know, the drug thing. That's always trouble."

"I can tell by how decent you are to me. She never gave you any details."

Ralph drew away. "Don't do this. You're good now. None of my business."

"Those prisoners of war." He shifted closer to Ralph, checked the station clock. "I think I know why they wanted to die."

"We're back on that?"

"They were cowards, and they knew it. Even if they were freed, every day for the rest of their lives, they were gonna know."

"Talk about something else, for crissake." Ralph stabbed a finger at him. "And it was better than being dead."

He snorted. "There's lots worse than dead, Ralph. Like a life with no chance of redemption. Once a person knows that, there's no way to fix it. Ever. Not drugs. Not counseling. Nothing."

"I don't like this, Mikey. Almost eleven. I'm gonna go. I want you to come with me."

"Wait. Let me ask you this. Do you think there are people who should kill themselves?"

"What?" Brow creased, Ralph peered into the dark. "No. It's a mortal sin. They'd go to hell."

"Wow, hell." Mike smiled, shook his head. "But what if it was to prevent a different kind of sin, a worse sin?"

"Mortal sin is mortal sin. Not like there's better or worse."

"See, I think that's wrong. I think some people are just bad, and they know it. And I think the first time they see the monster inside, they should jump off a building or put a bullet through their brain. Nobody would ever know why. Just them. Would take the guts of a hero to do that. God wouldn't send someone like that to hell. He'd smile on them for it."

Ralph stared at him. "You're staying with us tonight. Let's go," he said, pushing to his feet.

He snatched Ralph's shirt, yanked him back onto the bench. "You're going to tell Molly."

"Hey." Ralph elbowed the hand away, rolled his shoulders. "Where do you get off grabbing me?"

"Sorry," he said, both palms raised. "It's just … Ralph, you have a great heart. You'll tell her the right way."

"Come with me, and you can tell her."

"I tried to write it out, but this is better." He took a deep breath, checked the clock again. "When I got clean, especially from the meth, it took me a while to figure it out, but I finally did. See, I was never after a high. I needed to lose my mind, to hide." He slapped his chest. "There's a hole. I can't—" He grimaced, pounded a fist on his thigh. "See, this is why I couldn't write it out. It's not a hole. It's a … a black place. A defect. Buzzed or sober it's there. It'll always be there. Dangerous. Like a loose cobra in the house. I don't want to be afraid of it anymore."

"Jesus." Ralph rubbed his lips, flicked his eyes around the empty platform.

"I killed him."

"Killed who? Jeremy?" Ralph's face went blank. "You killed Jeremy?"

"The more I showed up, the worse he got."

"Oh, for crissake." Ralph's nose wrinkled. "Was the cancer. Had nothing to do with you."

"Yeah? What if he was like those prison camp guys? You know, afraid and hopeless all the time. Maybe he let the cancer take him."

"Here's what we're gonna do." Ralph pointed to the exit stairs. "We're going back to the house. Rosalie'll make us some coffee. You can—"

"Ralph, this is my last night on earth."

"What?" floated on a whisper.

"I've known for weeks this would be the right time."

"No, you're not."

"All the bad endings. Bunch 'em together. Get 'em over with."

"Ah, Jeez." Ralph grabbed twice for Mike's evading arm. "Come with me, Mikey. We'll go see someone. Right now. We'll go to the Emergency Room."

He sprang from the bench and skipped backward. "Said my piece. We're done."

"Mikey, please." Ralph pushed to his feet and plodded after him, arms extended. "You can't dump this on me."

"There's other things. Molly knows."

Ralph's pursuit slowed. "Gotta get past tonight. That's all. Things always seem worse at night. You musta seen that, huh? Mikey? Ever notice that?"

"Talk to Molly."

"Don't want to go to the hospital? Okay. We'll go home. Just home. I promise."

"Ask Molly how I was with him," he said, backing up, keeping the distance constant.

"You tell me," Ralph said, still scuffing toward him, "in the car."

He shoved both palms out. "Stand still, godammit!"

"Okay," Ralph said, arms raised in surrender. "Relax. But you gotta tell me. I'm supposed to understand something, right?"

"That's right." He turned sideways, left one arm extended, dropped his gaze to the concrete. "That's right." His arm lowered slowly. "Ralph, from the day Jeremy was born, I had nothing for him. Felt nothing. Drugs might have had something to do with it, but I don't think so. He was Molly's pet, her hobby. And then when he got sick, everything in our world, and I mean everything, became him. Little by little, I got to hate him."

"Bullshit. I was there. I saw."

"That's when I realized the wiring was bad," he said, tapping his chest. "Here's this little boy, sick as hell. My *son*, for crissake. And I hated him. Hated the sight of him, the sound of his voice, his nervous smile, always like someone had a camera stuck in his face." His eyes closed. "And the smell, that awful smell from the chemo—"

"Shut up."

"Bills we'd never pay. Molly in a zombie fog. Pointless toys and vid—"

"Shut up!"

"And I was sober then. When I was still using, it was worse. I hurt him."

"Hurt him how?" Ralph said, his expression blank.

"So loaded all the time I'm not sure. There's screaming, furniture going over, falling. Fuzzy clips and snapshots mostly. Except this one time." He squeezed his forehead, began to pace. "Can't see a face because her head's down. Y'know, like a bull ready to charge. Both her arms are reaching backward. She's yelling, 'You're not touching him.' It's so clear, and it's in my head so often, I can even see it from behind her, feel those little wrists in her grip, being pulled against her backside. Each twist and stumble nearly knocking him off his feet. She's screeching and growling. Slaps and punches are pouring in, but she never lets go. Never blocks one swing. Just takes it until the pounding runs out of steam."

Ralph glided a half-step closer, eyes narrowed, hands balled into fists. "You scumbag."

"No argument," he said, breathing hard. "Can't take it anymore."

Within striking distance, Ralph stopped and looked down. "No," he said softly. He shook his head in long, slow sweeps. "No," he said a bit louder. "I know you since you're ten. You couldn't do that. And she would've told someone. Us, the cops, someone."

"She got a restraining order, for crissake. I couldn't see them till I was clean for almost three months. You know me? Nobody knows anybody."

"You were crazy back then. Up on the roof. Watering the lawn naked. Throwing stuff at cars. She didn't want Jeremy to remember you like that. Nothing about beatings. She would've told us."

"I know what happened."

"Mikey, I'm telling you, you were nuts. And that goddam meth. Could still be playing tricks right now for all—"

"Stop!" He bounced his praying hands. "Ralph, I know what I know," he said, his tone calm, each word spoken slowly. "I'll always know. I have to do this."

"Let's go. Right now. We'll ask Molly. No, wait a sec." Ralph fumbled in his pocket and brought out a phone. "We'll call her." He punched some buttons and pointed the glowing phone toward Mike. "Look, I'm calling her. See? She'll tell you."

Over Ralph's shoulder, a faraway twinkling gleamed along the polished rails. Mike grabbed the phone. "Let her sleep," he said, ending the call. He blew out a long breath. "You may be right. Maybe if I talked to someone. Tell you what. Tomorrow, I'll call my sponsor. See what—"

"No. Right now. I'm useless. You gotta talk to someone who knows something about this."

He peeked at the tracks again, followed the glow to its source. "Tomorrow." His arm hooked Ralph's shoulder. "Let's go."

"Really?" Ralph's head slumped, knees buckled. "Thank God." Crying, he snapped Mike in a tight hug. "Been enough heartbreak for one day."

They slapped backs, disengaged, and headed for the stairwell to the parking lot.

"You got help on the drugs, Mikey," Ralph said as they clomped down the stairs. "You'll get this worked out, too."

"Ah, *crap.*" He slapped his pockets. "My phone. Probably fell out on the bench. Go ahead. Meet you at the car."

"I'll pull it around," Ralph yelled to his back.

"Gotcha," he said, bounding up the stairs two at a time. At the top he checked over his shoulder, watched

Ralph drop heavily onto each tread until he reached the bottom and disappeared.

Clanging and thunder rushed in front of the train as it entered the station. He dashed to the yellow border and turned away from the tracks. Arms crossed over his heart, he leaned back and dropped into the Cyclops glare.

RESTLESS

ONLY MINUTES PAST NOON and Manhattan's towers had already drawn a shadow across the canyon floor. Will pecked his wife on the lips at the cab's open door.

"It's not too late," she said, doodling a finger on his shoulder, "and you might even be hurting Courtney's feelings."

"Lorraine, enough. You both know I hate the beach, and I've already seen the little food processor."

"Our granddaughter's name is Amelia. Do you do that just to annoy me?"

"Early onset Alzheimer's. Go," he said, patting her bottom. "Bond."

She slapped his hand away and checked over both shoulders "What's wrong with you?"

"You'll miss your train. Call me tonight." He waved at the disappearing cab and returned to the apartment house lobby.

A uniformed woman smiled at him as she exited an oversized closet behind the security desk. "So, Mrs. Sinclair's gone to see the new baby for a week. Bachelor again, huh?"

Grinning, he angled toward the counter. "Got something in mind, Tanya?"

"Sure," she said, laughing. "How about dinner and a Broadway show? You, me, and my husband. And you pay for the sitter."

"Aw, you're no fun. I'm busy anyway. Tonight? Dinner at Le Canard. You know it?"

She crinkled her nose. "You kidding? KFC's a big night for us."

"Found it last summer in Soho. Great place. Small, but the whole front opens to the street. Terrific for watching the beautiful people." He bounced his eyebrows. "Like you."

"You can't be that desperate."

"Making a big mistake, Tanya. Gonna be great. Couple glasses of wine, steak au poivre. If you don't come, it's gonna be me, all alone at the bar, doing the *Sunday Times* puzzles."

"Sounds kind of sad, really."

"You're weakening. I can tell."

Frozen smile on her face, Tanya waved at another tenant coming off the elevator. "Your poor wife."

PENN STATION'S CHAOS behind her, Lorraine un-wound in a window seat. Scenery never became pastoral during the eastbound trip to Southampton, but at least the cubism of the city melted away. Eyes closed, she let the jostling train massage Manhattan from her system.

Despite the previous August, New York still felt extraterrestrial. Last year's month-long experiment with city living should have cured them both. The plan had been to immerse and find the gems, see if New York could be their post-retirement home. It exhausted her. Every meal taken in a restaurant, no repeats. Plays, museums, movies, comedy clubs, jazz clubs, galleries, ball games, Shakespeare in the Park, tours of everything. Eleven thousand on the Amex, all for kaleidoscopic memories and six new pounds.

This year, it was do-overs. Will acted as if this identified them as savvy insiders, rather than people out of ideas or initiative. To her, each new day cemented the city as foul-smelling, hostile, and absurdly expensive. More than ever, she knew living amid elephantine buildings — and people who treated her as invisible — would be a sub-basement in hell. At the end of last August, she thought she'd made it clear there would be no relocation, at least not one that included her, but here they were, trying it again. Just considering the possibility of another month next year tightened her face.

At the Jamaica stop, a middle-aged woman, speaker-buds in her ears, set a canvas carryall on the middle cushion and sat in the aisle seat. She made no eye contact and busied herself with knitting before the train left the station.

No one to blame but herself this year. She could have let him go alone and stayed in Larchmont. Tended the garden. Read. Ate simply and only when she wanted. Except there'd been all those years of catching him watch women. Not earthy and comedic like construction workers on lunch break. More like a man on the hunt, processing reactions, imagining things. And some women looked back, even if they saw he belonged to her. Brazen and challenging. Some looked even when he didn't. Corner of the eye glances. Ember of a smile on each pretty face, ready to flame if conditions turned favorable. She had no reason to suspect he'd ever acted on any of it, but a month of being vulnerable to such women held too much potential.

Even that upset her. Those possibilities should have been off the table by now. The two of them should have arrived at the cozy phase in their lives, a time when friendship blossomed as their glands withered. There was none of it. He pestered her more than ever for sex, frequently in ways she found degrading or deviant. It sharpened awareness of her decline, the widening chasm between her pleasures and his passions. She wasn't a dog or French whore. Why was she supposed to want to do those things now? Because he was bored? "I don't like it," she blurted.

The woman next to her removed an earbud, tilted her head closer, but continued to face forward. "You say something?"

"Sorry." She covered her mouth and chuckled. "Talking to myself. Must be getting old."

The woman nodded and stuck the earpiece back in.

WILL APPROACHED LE CANARD'S outdoor lectern. A top-heavy teenage hostess stood behind it, her jaw rolling on gum. Fingertips of each hand alternately stroked the summer-blond hair she'd pulled forward over one shoulder.

"Bar," he said, slowing at her station.

Hardly a nod. She leaned her folded arms onto the tilted surface, bubbling her breasts into the wide gap of a clingy top.

He claimed a seat at the twelve-seat mahogany bar. Glass of cabernet in hand, he glanced back at the hostess, still bent onto the lectern, still playing with her hair. The rear was just as provocatively packaged as the front and equally captivating. So much so, he was unaware of an arrival on the next stool until the woman clunked her gigantic purse onto the bar.

She ordered vodka on the rocks, dragged the bag onto her lap, and stuck her face inside. Hands scooped through what sounded like thousands of metal or plastic objects. "Where the hell is it?"

He couldn't place the accent.

"Dammit!" was followed by a flamenco tantrum on the footrest of her barstool. She re-entered the bag, far enough inside to muffle her voice. "Has to be here." She popped out of the bag and grasped his arm. "Do you have a phone?"

"Be my guest." He slipped his from a shirt pocket and handed it to her.

"I don't want yours. Call me."

"How would—"

She snatched his phone and punched in a number. The Rolling Stones song, *Bitch*, played inside her bag. "I knew it." She dove back in and emerged with a glowing cell phone.

"Interesting choice of ringtone," he said.

"Oh, you recognized it? A joke by my ex. Haven't gotten around to changing it."

"You seemed a little frantic," he said. "Expecting a call from the White House?"

"Hardly. A dear friend is coming into JFK from Israel tonight. This is the only number she has." A relaxed smile added more pretty to her face. She raised her drink to him. "Thank you. *Nastrovya*."

Each took a sip. He opened the *Sunday Times* magazine to the puzzles page and uncapped his ballpoint.

"I can't do those at all," she said, reorganizing whatever was inside her bag, "and you do them in ink? You must be a genius."

"They get easier after you've done them for years. And I'd have to think if English isn't your mother tongue, they could be damn near impossible."

She glanced at him and laughed. "So, you think I have an accent, yes?"

"You said your friend is coming in from Israel. Are you Israeli?"

"Russia first, then Israel. You'd think after twenty years in New York I'd speak American, but no." She tapped the edges of her black, mid-neck hair and tipped her face to the ceiling. "Of course, I was only two at the time." She took the pen from him, capped it, and tossed it onto the magazine. "Don't do that damn thing. Keep me company while I wait for my call. Everyone calls me Cee," she said, holding out her hand, "like the letter."

"Will Sinclair."

"You live in Manhattan, Will?" Eyes on him, she took a long sip of her drink.

"Westchester. But I keep a sublet on West 74th. You?"

"So," she said, pointing to his gold band, "you're married. Or is that to frighten away wicked women?"

He swiveled toward her. "The truly wicked wouldn't care."

"Are you?"

"Sometimes."

"Oh, that's so funny. Me too." She held up three fingers

during a slurp of vodka. "Three times," she said, glass poised at her lips. "And you?"

"Just once."

She rolled her eyes and set the glass on the bar. "So, where's your wife tonight?"

"Visiting relatives."

"How do you know she's not doing what you're doing?"

He smiled. "And what am I doing, exactly?"

"When you said 'sometimes' that means you cheat. Men who cheat are gutless." Sneer on her face, she crawled cat paws on the bar. "All that sneaking around and lying. For what? If there's nothing left, just end it."

"Who the hell—" He twisted away from her and uncapped his pen. "Nice talking to you."

"Don't." She grasped the wrist of his pen hand. "I'll be nice. Just a little jumpy right now. So," she said, patting the back of his hand, "why don't you tell me some more about yourself? What do you do?"

He studied her briefly before setting the pen down. "Nothing. Sold my software company last year. That's how I can do the sublet thing. Got the time. Got the money. Why not, right?"

"How old are you?"

"Wow." He laughed. "Do you have even a nodding acquaintance with the concept of small talk?"

"Stupid waste of time. And don't tell me how old. I'm good at this." She squinted through a slow once-over. "Let's see, mostly gray. Some lines around the eyes and mouth. No spots on the hands yet. Posture's still good. Fairly trim. Boring shirt and slacks. Brown deck shoes, no socks." She slumped and eyeballed him for a few more seconds. "Fifty-one."

"Missed by a mile. Thirty-three."

"Oh, bullshit."

"Fifty-two."

The passing bartender nodded at Will's open-book gesture.

"Mind if I try that with you?" Will said to her.

"You're a brave one," she said, eyebrows raised. "Go ahead, but I won't admit it even if you're right. Wait." She tossed and fluffed her hair, tucked her red, candy-striped blouse tighter into a black leather skirt, and rolled her shoulders one at a time. "Okay. Ready."

"Turn toward me a little." He used his thumb like a gun sight. "So, we've got a few character lines around the eyes. Lips still full. Tight skin at the jaw and neck. Good, uh, elevation we'll call it. Quite slender. Stylish clothes. Great legs. Sensible flats." He folded his arms and released a long exhale through his nose while he stared at her. "I'm gonna say … nineteen."

Smiling, she slapped both hands to her cheeks and batted her lashes. "My God, how did you do that?" Drink poised near her lips, she peered over the rim and lost her smile. "But not so brave after all." As the bartender bustled past, she stopped him with a loud hum into her vodka and a finger jabbing at her glass.

The barman nodded and hurried off.

"Wait," she called after him, "this man just asked for a menu. Bring two." She squeezed Will's hand. "The smell of those steaks is making me hungry. Shall we order something while I wait for my call?"

"Sounds great." He turned off his phone.

"LEAVE HER, HONEY." Sitting at the kitchen table, Lorraine angled a shoulder to shield the baby from her daughter's reaching arms. "She's fine."

Courtney eased the sleeping infant from her. "Mom," she said, chuckling, "you still have six more days."

"Didn't realize how much I miss it." She watched her daughter cradle, dance, and coo the tiny bundle to a bassinet in the master bedroom. As if empowered by a Dickens ghost, she saw herself tending to Courtney twenty-six years earlier. Wistfulness and envy. Joy and loss. Pride and regret. Confusion.

Courtney clicked the bedroom door shut and tiptoed back to the kitchen. "Lots of frowning tonight," she said, running water over their dinner dishes. "Everything okay?"

"Was I?" She joined her daughter at the sink. "Sit, honey. I'll do that." She grabbed a sponge and nudged her daughter to the side.

"Thanks." Courtney stayed next to her, backside resting against the counter. "God," she said, hands covering her face, "she'll be up again in three hours. Okay if I get some sleep?"

"Hmm? Sure. Go ahead."

"Mom, where *are* you tonight?"

She bounced her shoulders and forced a smile. "Just tired. Your father's summer odyssey is a bit too whirlwind for me. Soon as I finish here, I'm going to turn in, too."

"Whoopee," Courtney said, laughing, "*Girls Gone Wild* made it all the way to nine o'clock." She laid her head on Lorraine's shoulder. "I'm so glad you're here. With Michael in China, this week would have been impossible. Thank you."

"Get some sleep," she said, tilting her head until it touched Courtney's.

Kitchen cleanup finished, she crept outside and strolled toward the rhythmic thuds of the ocean. Several doors from Courtney's rental, she took out her phone and called Will.

Voicemail.

"Hi, honey," she said. "Guess you're at dinner or in bed. Arrived safe and sound. Had a terrific day. Women and babies. What could be better, right? Tomorrow's supposed to be perfect. If you're out and get home before 10:00, gimme a jingle. Love ya. Wish you were here."

CEE'S ARMS WRAPPED ABOVE Will's elbow as they tottered toward La Casa Bonita, a Cuban jazz club on First Street. She'd suggested they go there near the end of dinner, after her second glass of Cabernet. The evening was far too steamy for the closeness, but her breast frequently brushed or squished against his arm. A new-woman delight he hadn't experienced since college. Based on the variety of directions she pulled, he suspected her arm hugs were more for stability than a progressing familiarity.

"Will, they have the most wonderful music at this place. If you're going to spend time in Manhattan, these are the spots to find." A muffled tune thumped inside her bag. In the dark, she had no trouble finding her phone. Palm pushed at him, she checked the display and wandered away a few strides. "Terrific," was all he heard clearly. She danced back to him, arms swaying over her head. "Yes," hissed through her teeth.

"Your visitor's here?"

A puzzled look passed quickly. She shook her head. "Even better. My dealer's out on bail. I just scored us some coke. He's at La Casa Bonita right now." She grabbed his arm again. "C'mon, left foot, right foot. I was in the Israeli army when I was eighteen. March with me, soldier. It'll be fun. Let's go, double time."

His legs moved like they were in braces. "I don't know about this."

She dragged him like a reluctant St. Bernard. "C'mon, move. It's safer if a man goes with me."

"Wait. Why are we doing this if it's dangerous? Just have him come to your apartment."

She tugged harder. "How would that be safer? And this isn't Chinese take-out, for godsake. Let's go. I'm out and he's waiting."

"I've never done coke," he said, still tolerating some forward motion. "Not even much weed. Let's just go—" He yanked his elbow loose. "How stupid can I be? There's no one coming into JFK."

"What? Of course there is. She'll be calling any minute." Cee snatched his arm. "C'mon."

Again, he spun free. Arms folded, he leaned against a light post and shook his head.

"Nothing bad can happen," she said. "We go in. I pay him. He gives me the coke, and we go back to my apartment."

"People have died. First time, and they died. I'd call that bad."

"Good God," she said, one hand covering her eyes. "You're not going to die." She sidled closer and smiled. "I'll show you. Do what I do, and you'll be fine." Stretching onto tiptoes, she slipped her arms around his neck. "And if you die, so what? Everyone dies. Have a little fun first, yes?" Her hands slid to his butt and pulled her grinding hips against him. "I promise you," she whispered, "if you take me to *La Casa Bonita*, you're going to want to be with me afterward."

He swallowed and pushed away from the pole.

They trekked a few blocks through the Lower East Side's "alphabet city." Outposts of gentrification materialized now and then, but the night was mostly populated by young Hispanic men and women, driven from tenement apartments by the swelter. Sidewalks and stoops rang with Spanish music, shouts, and laughter. He avoided eye contact as they slalomed through, giving the widest berth to young women who danced to the boom-box rhythms, their wrists propped on wriggling, rolling hips. Coy smiles for the eager-eyed men clapping and shouting encouragement.

"I see why you wanted an escort," he said when they reached the soaped-up door of *La Casa Bonita*.

She poked a thumb over her shoulder. "Them? Don't be stupid. They're just having fun. The danger's in here," she said, pointing to the door.

"What? How?"

"Maybe someone sees something," she said with a shrug. "They follow me. Next thing, they've got my money and the coke. That won't happen with you along." She pulled the door open. "At least I don't think so. Ah, there he is. C'mon. I'll buy you a *Cuba libre*."

MOONLIGHT GLOWED on the kitchen table where Lorraine sat in front of her dark phone and cup of cold tea.

Sounds of baby fussing in Courtney's bedroom were followed by a band of light spilling under her door. When her daughter didn't come out, Lorraine tiptoed to the door and knocked.

"C'mon in." Courtney lounged against a pillow, the baby angled onto her breast. "Did she wake you? Sorry."

"I was up. Just wanted another peek before turning in. G'night, honey." She pulled at the knob.

"Mom, wait. Keep me company." She inched sideways and patted the bed. "Tell me about the city. You never say what you're doing. My friends think it's fabulous."

"Fabulous alright." She smiled and sat on the bed's edge, fingertips smoothing the baby's sparse hair. "Guess I enjoy some of it, but I miss my routines. Your dad seems to need something different all the time, but I like my quiet life. I belong there."

"What about here?"

She rubbed the baby's back. "Just what I needed right now. It'll probably give me a better attitude when I go back. As they say, absence makes the heart blah, blah, blah. Right? Let him skitter around for a couple more weeks, then it's back to normal." She kissed her fingers, touched them to the baby's head and Courtney's cheek. "Time for bed."

CEE HUNG ON Will's arm as they left *La Casa Bonita*. "You," she said, laughing and wagging a finger in his face, "are a terrible dancer."

"Told you I'm no good." He squeezed her hand. "I'm

curious. When you went to the lady's room …" He tapped a thumb under each nostril.

"Tiny bit."

"Figured." He patted the fingers clamped around his elbow. "So, want to know my theory about dancing?"

Her feet and hips popped into action. "God, I love to dance."

"I think dancing was invented by women, for women. Gives them a chance to challenge each other, to advertize." He shook the arm she was holding. "I liked what you were selling." He rocked his hips and shoulders.

"Stop," she said, grimacing. "People looking out the window will call an ambulance. How could such a clumsy man ever get a woman?"

Statue-still on the dance floor, as their instructor insisted, he holds Lorraine's fingers over his head. She twirls around him. Let's go. Wedding dress hiked to her thighs, she circles. Offers and teases. Eyes glittering, she backs away. Hips and shoulders churning, she inches toward him. Fingers curl and beckon. He walks into an embrace. Women squeal and men hoot. He smells her perfume and hairspray. She holds his face. Kisses his mouth. He feels the tacky slick of her lipstick. Tastes the wine on her tongue.

"Thought you said you lived close?" he said, rubbing his eyes.

"One more block." She raised her eyebrows and smiled. "Nervous?"

"A little."

"First time's always exciting though, yes?"

"Who said this is my first time?"

"You did. 'I don't do coke', you said. Are you drunk?" Bass notes bumped inside her bag. She dug out the phone and cupped a hand over her ear. "Milaya! You're here?" Pleasure lit her face. "Fantastic, and you have the address … Okay, jump in a cab, and I'll see you in about an hour." She smacked a kiss into the phone. "Me too. *Ciao.*"

They scuffed up the steps of her brownstone. "Milaya," he said. "Is she as beautiful as her name?"

"She's spectacular. And Milaya's not her name. It's Russian for 'my pretty one'." Cee unlocked the door and pushed on his back. "You have twenty minutes." Pausing in the small vestibule, he watched contents of her handbag cascade onto a glass coffee table. She kicked off her shoes and waved him into the room. "Want a drink or something?" she said, dropping to her knees and opening the bag of coke.

"Let's just do this."

LORRAINE FLIPPED ON THE LIGHT in the bathroom. She stood at the sink, appalled at how the undersized bulb lit her face. Raccoon eyes, nose elongated by shadow, vertical trenches in her upper lip. "God," she whispered, "I'm a ghoul." Firm swipes of a wet washcloth removed foundation and color. She swirled in blobs of moisturizer, pausing occasionally to stretch skin toward her ears. Maybe next year she'd get the lift. Couldn't have strangers mistaking her for his mother. Except that would be better than a botch. Better than turning out like those pathetic women who looked like praying mantises or fire victims. Maybe two more years. She frowned at the reflection again and turned off the light.

Sleep wouldn't come. She punched and hugged the pillow, kicked and yanked at the covers. Her eyes hurt but wouldn't stay closed. She grabbed her phone from the nightstand and checked the face. 11:21. A quick scroll through *inbox* and *missed calls* confirmed Will hadn't phoned. She re-set the ringtone to vibrate and laid it on the empty side of the bed.

JUST SHORT OF MIDNIGHT, Will stood at a window in their sublet. Lights out, hair nearly dry, he watched figures scurrying twenty-four stories below. So many people. Had to be a few who strayed tonight. He wondered if they were bursting to share details, or if they trudged in private loathing, resolved to no repeats. Guilty men probably showered soon as they got home, even if the apartment was empty. Scrubbed away the scents of attraction and the pungency of success. Maybe threw their underwear down the trash chute.

Still a little jacked from his first ever hit of coke, a "gutless" amount, he crawled into bed and turned his back to the empty pillow, relieved Lorraine wasn't there. She might have detected something before the shower. Something on his clothes, or hands, or face. Maybe asked a question that made him avoid her eyes, and even if nothing more was said, each would know the other knew.

GONE

NOT POSSIBLE, not at this hour. Just short of their driveway, early morning sunlight glowed orange on the unpaved Georgia road. Mark slowed the car to a stop alongside knee-high weeds. Leaving the door ajar, he shuffled to the front bumper and gawked across the culvert to his farm's denuded slopes. For the first time ever, he could see the house and barn, riding atop a hill, now surrounded by a vast five-o'clock shadow of stumps.

The passenger door opened. "My God," Lizbeth said. His wife's slow stride swished and snapped through the brush until both her hands gripped his elbow. "What the hell happened?"

"Let's go." Behind the wheel again, he handed her his phone. "Try Glenda."

"C'mon, honey," Lizbeth said after dialing their daughter, "pick up … pick up … Dammit, voicemail."

Their SUV fishtailed up sharp twists in the quarter-mile driveway and arrived at a wide, pea-gravel parking area between the house and barn. Skidding to a stop surrounded the car in a thick fog of stone dust.

"She's got company," he said, pointing at two vehicles parked beside the barn. One was the black and gold Mini

Cooper they'd bought Glenda last year as a graduation present. The other was a black Cadillac Escalade, the kind with a rear end like a pickup truck. Still had the dealer sticker on the window.

"Climb over here after I get out," he said. "Leave it running."

"You're scaring me," she said, holding out his phone. "Should we call 911?"

"Punch it in, I guess, but don't send it unless something happens."

"What does that mean? What's 'something'?"

"How do I know?" As soon as he opened the car door, he heard O'Keeffe, the Newfoundland they'd bought Glenda for protection. The dog raged from inside the barn, banging and scratching at the door. Directly above the dog's outburst, in a window of the converted loft, he spied their only child. Glenda stood in partial shadow, a smile on her slender, oval face. Out of college now, but still as delicate and fragile as a pre-teen. One hand clutched a robe together at her throat, the other flapped at him like a baby.

"It's okay," he shouted over his shoulder to Lizbeth. Glenda's placid smile calmed him, but not a lot. Destruction had swirled around her, probably for days, without any outbound contact. Before Mark could shout a question about his stolen forest, a man intruded into the window. A gangster Jesus. Gaunt, bearded, shirtless. Dark hair to his shoulders. Unsmiling, the man hung an arm around Glenda's neck and scanned the courtyard.

Lizbeth's steps crunched gravel until she stopped next to him. A quick peek at her startled eyes and wide-stretched frown said she'd seen the man, too.

Glenda cranked open a panel of the casement window. Head against the man's chest, she circled her arms around his waist. "Hi, guys," she said, her words slow and tuneful. "Why are you here?"

"Honey," he yelled up to her, "what the hell happened? How could you not call us?"

"C'mon up," she said. "Someone I want you to meet." She nuzzled into the bare chest.

The man released Glenda and receded into the dark.

"Glenda, answer me."

She peeked over her shoulder, glanced back at them, and drew the curtains.

"This is nuts," he said, grabbing Lizbeth's hand and hurrying to the metal, exterior staircase

Midway to the top, the apartment door banged open. The man, shoving his arm into the sleeve of a denim jacket, stumbled onto the landing. Cold enough for steam breath, but he still had no shirt on. His ribs aligned like railroad ties. Smiling, but never meeting their eyes, he turned sideways and danced past.

"Where you going?" Mark said, reaching for him.

"One second," the man said in a hoarse baritone, index finger raised above his shoulder. His steps and voice drew snarls and thumps from behind the barn door. Stutter-stepping away from the dog's fury, he broke into a trot and disappeared around the corner.

"Hey," Mark hollered, "want to talk to you."

The Escalade started up.

Lizbeth hooked Mark's arm when he lunged down the stairs. "Are you crazy?" she said as the SUV sped past, the man's face turned away from them.

He shook free and stared at the rooster tail of dust snaking down the driveway.

"C'mon," Lizbeth said, tugging his arm. "Let's get up there and see what she has to say."

Glenda stepped barefoot onto the metal landing, both hands scrunching the thin robe to her throat. "So you met—" Her mouth and eyes jumped wide. Feet tiptoed in place. "Omigod!" She darted back through the open door.

As they neared the top step, smells of food going funky escaped through the open doorway. "Leave it open," Lizbeth said as she passed him on the way inside.

Took a second to adjust to the dim light, but every cranny that came into focus was a chaos of plates, Chinese food cartons, pizza boxes, clothing, beer cans, glasses, and silverware. Flipping on the overhead in the kitchenette only magnified the mess.

Face flushed, Glenda rushed to them in half-steps and lurches. Each got a quick hug and kiss. "So, you met my angel, Gabriel." She hunched her shoulders and giggled. "Just love saying that."

"What in God's name is going on?" Lizbeth said, eyeballing the squalor. "And why is O'Keeffe—"

"O'Keeffe," Mark shouted. "The trees. What happened to the trees?"

Glenda's dreamy gaze stayed on Lizbeth. "She attacks Gabriel when he's doing me."

Tingling chased around Mark's face and neck.

"I get kinda loud," Glenda said, wrinkling her nose. "Must confuse her. So, she gets the barn, and I get him." Eyes closed, she tipped her face to the ceiling. "My beautiful, magical genius." She threw an arm out and steadied herself. "He's so great," she said, blinking and smiling.

Lizbeth rested both arms on Glenda's shoulders. She studied their daughter's face, sniffed her nose and mouth. "Are you drunk?"

"Nooo," Glenda said through a covered chuckle.

A sick airiness filled his head and stomach. "Drugs?" he said.

"Listen to me." Lizbeth's firm shake wobbled Glenda's head. "We're about to call the police about the trees. If you're on something, they're going to know it. And if there's anything here, they're going to find it."

"Daddy, don't." Glenda shook her head in long, slow sweeps. "There was no food. We just like *borrowed* the trees. Gabriel found people. I signed some papers. Don't be mad." She flapped a hand at him. "They'll grow back."

He quick-tallied what was taken. Most of the trees were longleaf pine, but the black walnuts along the stream had to fetch thousands each. Gabriel's haul was in the middle six figures. "Where's the money?"

Glenda snorted and nodded. "He was right. Money." Pale eyes wandering, she glanced a finger off the tip of her nose. "Stinks of money."

"How do you even know that derelict?" he said.

"Fences? Guard dogs?" Nose crinkled, Glenda flipped a hand toward the outside. "For trees?" She leaned closer to him. "For God's trees?"

He needed to still his hands. "What was he doing here? Who is he?"

"Same with me," Glenda said. "Shut away up here."

"You *begged* to come here." Lizbeth said.

Glenda punched a finger at him. "One of your trees."

He glanced at Lizbeth, hoping the crease in her brow meant she was close to figuring something out.

"Well," Glenda said, a sleepy smile pulling at her lips, "you're too late."

"We've wasted enough time." He marched to the phone and snatched the handset from the cradle. "Does 'angel' Gabriel have a last name?"

Glenda laid her face on Lizbeth's shoulder. "Don't let him, Momma. They'll grow back. Nature's perfect."

"If that isn't the stup—" He stalked back toward her, phone raised like a club. "Is that what your dirtbag said? Nature's perfect? I'm gonna spend the rest of my life in a goddam wasteland, and that's it? Nature's perfect?"

Lizbeth jumped between him and Glenda. "How's that helping?" she said, glaring over a shoulder.

"But she—" His body trembled. "Why do you always do this?"

Arms draped loosely around her mother's neck, Glenda spied at him from the corners of her eyes "If you saw the scars, Momma." She pointed to her legs. "He needs the Oxy."

"So it's OxyContin?" Lizbeth said.

Glenda nodded.

"And why do you need it?" he said.

She laid her cheek on Lizbeth's shoulder. "Neck. Too much ..." Her arm pantomimed stiff-arm painting stokes.

"Bull. Where's the rest?"

"Daddy, he's coming right back. There's no food," she said, her voice rising to a squeaky sob. "Please, just wait."

"He's not coming back, you idiot." He punched in 911.

Struggling to break free from Lizbeth, Glenda screeched "hang up" throughout his conversation with the police. Soon as the call ended, she collapsed onto Lizbeth's shoulder and cried softly.

"The dispatcher said they're busy with an accident on Rte 94, but someone should be here within the hour. I gave them a description of that bastard's truck." He poked his chin toward Glenda. "Maybe she'd come around faster if she got cleaned up a little."

"C'mon, honey," Lizbeth said, stroking Glenda's hair, "let's get you into the shower." The two women headed for the far end of the apartment, where a queen-sized bed sat opposite the bathroom. They selected an outfit from clothes strewn on the floor. At the bathroom door, Glenda's eyes found him. Tears dripped down her face. "Why do you like hurting people?" she said, sounding little again.

He pointed into the bathroom. "Take a good look in the mirror. I'm not the one hurting you."

Her head twitched, like she'd caught herself dozing.

"And stop thinking that loser's coming back. He's already got everything he could. G'won, get yourself cleaned up. The police will be here soon."

She whirled, heaved her clothes into the bathroom, and stumbled after them. The door slammed.

Lizbeth strode toward him, eyes huge. "Do you believe this? Any of it? When were we here last? Three weeks?"

"Big mistake letting her live out here. I should have said no."

"Excuse me?" She swept her arms at the four exposures of windows and the high ceiling. "If I recall, you were the one who said this place had 'perfect light' for a painter. I was the—" She shook her head. "We're not doing this now. And it was right to give her the chance."

"Have you lost your mind, too? Look around." He pointed to the studio end of the apartment. "Not even a blank canvas on an easel. Two months. Nothing. And that 'perfect light'? Every curtain is closed."

Eyes drifting around the dim apartment, she nodded. Her fingers jumped to her lips. "And omigod, what about O'Keeffe attacking when—"

"Lizbeth!" Ears covered, he hurried to the nearest window. "Let's get some air in here." He yanked a curtain open.

Seen from above, the new vista horrified and fascinated, like an amputation. Their endless blanket of cool green, replaced by spiky stumps in the flame-colored Georgia clay. Chimneys of a burnt city.

The bathroom door crashed into a wall. Glenda staggered out wearing blue jeans and a red sweatshirt, dark around the neckline because her hair was still dripping. She weaved toward her bed. Clothes fluttered as she kicked through them. Arms out like a wire walker, she slipped into a pair of slides. She grabbed her purse from the floor. Head tilted back, she tucked the bag under her arm and headed toward the door.

"No." He stepped between her and the exit. "You're not going anywhere."

"I'm twenty-one." She began to circle him.

He grabbed her arm and pointed to a sofa. "You're waiting for the police. Sit down."

"Gonna see O'Keeffe."

"You need your purse to play with the dog?"

"Don't want you going through my stuff."

"Open it," he said, pointing to the purse.

Glenda angled her slight body and bumped a shoulder into his chest. "I'm twenty-one. Move."

He reached behind her, snatched the handbag, and turned his back to her.

"You can't do that!"

"No prescription bottles," he said, raking through the contents while Glenda slapped and pounded his back. "No car keys, either." He turned and offered her the bag. "Okay, let's go see your dog."

"Me," she said, panting. "Not you." Her thumb bounced off her chest. "Just me."

Lizbeth patted his shoulder on her way to the sink with a stack of grungy plates. "There's no point. Let her go."

Glenda slammed the outside door shut. "O'Keeffe," she sang from the landing, "it's mommy." Frantic woofs and whines arose from below. Footsteps gonged in erratic bunches as she descended, followed by the barn door grumbling in its track.

Standing at the window, he saw the gigantic dog bound into mid-morning sunshine. She danced in leaping rings around Glenda who'd raised a fist over her head. Weaving toward the corner of the barn, she peeked up at the window, smiled, and baby-flapped her fingers.

He waved back.

A throwing motion sent O'Keeffe on a false chase. Bent over laughing, she staggered in pursuit until they both disappeared.

The Mini Cooper started.

"Lizbeth, she's leaving!" He reached the bottom of the

stairs in time to watch the tiny car cruise past, O'Keeffe in hot pursuit. His daughter looked straight ahead, lips curled in a smile. One hand poked high out of the driver's window, middle finger extended.

"CAN'T STAND THIS ANYMORE," Mark said. "O'Keeffe," he called out on his way to the hall closet, "go for a walk?"

The jumbo dog struggled to her feet in stages. Nails clicked on the hardwood as she trotted to join him. "Back soon," he said, slipping an arm into his jacket. "I want to take a look around before it's too dark. You're welcome to join us."

"She's gonna call." Lizbeth flipped a page of her magazine. "Or the police will."

"Don't you want to see what they did?"

"I'm only worried about Glenda right now. Go if you want." Another page crinkled. "Going to the stream?"

He nodded. "Although I'm not sure I want to. Come for me if anyone calls."

Gauzy clouds along the horizon permitted light from the setting sun, but no heat. Hands jammed into his jacket pockets, collar lifted against his neck, he kicked through trimmed branches littering the well-worn path. O'Keeffe ran ahead, fell behind, or trotted next to him. Every few steps of a new exploration she'd pause and find him before seeking the next.

The trail led to what had been his most treasured spot on the farm, a secluded clearing along a shallow stream. Despite winter's cold, his mind went to the pleasures of early summer. Even on cloudless days, a shield of hardwood leaves deflected all but the stealthiest darts of light. He'd lie on the cool earth, dangle his bare feet in the trickle. Toxins of the spirit, accumulated during sixty-hour workweeks, drained into the massaging waters. Frequently, he fell asleep.

When he saw it now, the little river was an open gash. He squatted on the bank, shut his eyes, and tried to summon the pleasantness. All he could picture was what he'd just seen, a despoiled orange ribbon, fouled fluid dribbling through a mesh of branches, leaves, and shriveled vines.

He gripped the jacket tight around his throat and headed back. O'Keeffe galloped ahead, all the way to the house. Sun was behind him now. No glow in his eyes to fuzz the clarity. Ahead, his long shadow dipped and darted in the path's irregularities. At each reluctant lift of the eyes, his violated property weighed more heavily, slowing his progress home until he stood immobile. In all directions, patient, indifferent specks of green – Glenda's promised restitution from "perfect Nature" – peeked through the Martian red.